Defying Gravity

Damaged Series
Book Two

Barrett

Affinity E-Book Press NZ LTD

Defying Gravity

2012 © Barrett

Affinity E-Book Press NZ LTD
Canterbury, New Zealand

ISBN- 13: 978-0615612904
ISBN- 10: 0615612903

Editor: Patty G. Henderson
Cover Design: Helen Hayes
Photo Credit: John Wills

Acknowledgements

It's hard to believe that within days of the release of my very first published novel, I began the revisions of book two. The past six months have flown by and almost without exception; I have worked every single day to try to make this book better than the first.

I needed to do it—not only for those who took a chance on my fledgling effort and me as an author, but to prove to myself that I had learned a thing or two in the process.

Honestly, it's been harder than I thought because the bar is set higher. I know these characters even better and feel more driven to share their journey.

With that in mind, I am extremely grateful for the support and feedback I have received from many of the readers, especially those of you who have shared your stories about your own personal struggles with PTSD. You are courageous.

I want to thank Amanda Speed for sticking with me since the very first version (which I'm sure was dreadful). Because of her familiarity and her eagle eye, she was able to provide me with some wonderful insights and suggestions. Thank you, Speed.

My critique partner, Cathy Rowlands, has steadfastly worked through minuscule details and confronted me whenever I needed a kick in the pants. She asked the hard questions that brought me a clearer vision of my character's motivations and more importantly, the underlying story I was trying to convey. Thank you.

Again, I want to thank the team at Affinity eBooks for believing in my vision and my story. Thanks to Mel, Julie, Nancy, and Patty for helping publish, what I hope will be a worthy successor to "Damaged in Service".

And finally, for my dear friend Kayce, for her continued support and encouragement, even more so when I didn't believe I could fly. Thank You.

Dedication

I dedicate this second book in the series to all of the men and women who serve daily protecting our lives, liberties, and freedom. This applies doubly for those individuals denied those same liberties and freedoms granted the very citizens they protect.

Chapter One

FBI Field Office
Chicago, Illinois
October

Zeke splashed cold water on her face and watched helplessly as both hands shook. The tremor started deep inside and surged out to her arms and legs like a tsunami. Her breathing was shallow and ragged and her skull threatened to explode from the expanding pressure. To stave off the impending panic while glowering at the disheveled image in the mirror, she clenched her jaw while a barrage of barely contained thoughts rumbled forth. Her fingers curled around the edge of the sink as her other hand scooped up the cold running water. The shock to her overheated skin seemed to ground her and sharpen her focus. She sucked in a large breath of air and held it before exhaling slowly.

It was during last night's drive from O'Hare into the city that the damn PTSD symptoms began to resurface. Fatigue and irritation jostled for supremacy just below the surface—nothing she tried had helped.

The three weeks she had spent away from Chicago, in New Mexico, had helped to ease the persistent tension, irritability, mood changes, and chilling fear. The wrenching pressure in her chest had relinquished some of its control. In its place, a pleasurable lightness burrowed into her hardened heart—the source: an amazing and beautiful woman. A quick smile of remembrance helped to smooth the tight creases in her face.

Zeke ran a wet hand through her hair a couple of times and shook her head. At least it looked better than it had before, she thought. She grabbed paper towels and resolved to shake off the ghosts that continued to linger. Her eyes traced to the blazer hanging on the door handle and she glanced at the white business envelope poking from the pocket. More than ever, she was determined to make some major life changes. After tossing the paper towel in the trash bin, Zeke looked at the reflection in the mirror again. The previously crisp white shirt hung lifelessly from weary shoulders. She put on the blazer and straightened the shirt collar before opening the door.

†

The small conference room reeked of stale coffee, hot electronic equipment, and male perspiration. Zeke twisted her head each side and groaned as her neck and shoulder muscles uncoiled.

She sat down, opened the file on her computer, and reread the report. It contained all of the pertinent data they had uncovered from the interrogation notes, plus their analysis and conclusions. It took another five minutes to finish her summary, which she saved to an encrypted file on the main server before forwarding it to another team leader. *What a clusterfuck! I've wasted five friggin' hours poring over phone logs, money trails, op reports, and endless arguments, and for what.* Zeke stood up and paced the length of the room. Her skin felt crawly, the way it always did when she'd missed something. She hated that feeling.

"Why is Ahmed's brother, Hassan, making my life hell? What does he think I can do? Shit. I told his damn hired thug where the brother was and he still beat me half to death." Zeke punched the metal post with the heel of her hand.

She leaned on one of the windowsills in the conference room and watched the tiny metal boxes crawling along below wondering if they carried the answer. *Reopening this case will probably be a huge waste of time and money.*

After the unusually long morning session, Zeke felt satisfied with the report they would give the boss after lunch. It didn't have all the answers she wanted but provided a solid basis for follow-up. The guys on her team had decided to go for Italian, but Zeke wasn't up to the normal testosterone-fueled brag-fest. Fortunately, the receptionist volunteered to bring her a sandwich.

She dug her cell phone out of her jacket pocket, turned it on, exited the conference room, and walked down the empty hall to the large waiting room nearby. *No messages.* The building noises, the conversation, and sounds of computer keyboards tapping diminished during the lunch hour. A low hum from the fluorescent light fixture ballasts and the whirring of the HVAC system created a hypnotic kind of white noise.

Once she flexed her arms, stretched out her back, and shoulders the tension dissipated. Several large tinted windows in the waiting room faced north toward the suburbs and a loud sigh escaped from deep inside Zeke as she took in the view on this unusually clear fall day. To the right she could see the recognizable and impressive skyline of the city proper. That sight had inspired any number of artists and she could see why— it was beautiful. The famed Chicago lakefront provided beauty, entertainment, and an unparalleled view. From this vantage point at least, no one could see the raw underbelly and the sinister side streets infested with decay. Zeke shivered hoping those frightening visions would fade.

She remembered her first sight of the famed Chicago skyline. Her three-year stint in the FBI's Chicago field office had started on a high note. Her new team had welcomed her, and thanks to everything falling into place, they made some quick arrests in several difficult cases. The Special Agent in Charge, Frank Hartbrooke, took her under his wing and allowed her to take extra career building cases that moved her up the ladder. Things changed when they received the case from hell.

The boss assigned her to a joint operation with the Chicago Police Department on a difficult murder case. They needed a new face to work undercover to track a methodical and ruthless serial killer. The last few months of the assignment turned into a nightmare, one she had recently fled from in order to breathe. After only a few weeks, her combination vacation and medical leave halted when she got the call to return to Chicago. The case she thought she closed reared its ugly head again.

The meager contents in her stomach churned like a cement mixer filled with battery acid that was eating her from inside out. She popped a couple of antacids from her pocket and watched cumulus clouds float over the city toward the lake.

Her mind drifted to the slower pace, clean air, and bright sunshine she'd left behind in New Mexico. The uncommon atmosphere of the southwest enchanted her. She felt a little smile form on her lips. What had begun as a two-month tour of the southwest had become *much* more interesting. New Mexico happily lived up to the slogan—*Land of Enchantment*.

The vibration of her cell phone brought her back to the present. "Cabot".

"Hi, can you talk?"

Anne's voice surprised and delighted her as a tingle shot down her spine. "Hi, Annie, perfect timing. How are you?" Sensuous warmth spread through her body, like velvety hot cocoa on a cold winter night.

"I'm really lonesome and wanted to hear your sexy southern drawl. I need to head over to Susan's later, but I wanted to thank you for the beautiful flowers you sent me."

Zeke relaxed and moved to one of the seating groups in the corner. "I'm glad you liked them. I was kind of hoping you'd think of me every time you looked at them."

"I already do that whenever I feel your wonderful necklace hanging between my breasts."

At the mention of Anne's breasts, a gentle fluttering started in Zeke's chest. "I miss you. I could hardly sleep last night."

"Might be a good idea to finish up your business and hurry back where you belong," Anne said.

"And where might that be?"

"You know perfectly well, nestled snugly between—my—sheets."

Zeke groaned. "You are a cruel mistress."

"I sincerely hope I'm more than a 'mistress'," Anne said.

"You are, believe me, you are," Zeke said.

A tall, heavyset woman walked toward her carrying a square Styrofoam container. It was the receptionist with Zeke's lunch.

"I guess I need to go now. I'll call you later, okay?"

"Take care, love you, Zeke."

†

Maywood, Illinois looked like the real Middle America. Tidy suburban homes set closely together with small well-tended yards. It looked like 'Anytown, USA'. Zeke drove down the tree lined street heading for her friend T.J.s' house for dinner. Instead of her normal special-agent-observations, she found herself looking at the scene differently. *This is probably the way most Americans live. In their small communities in homes with families and their regular every day jobs. What have I been doing all these years?*

Whenever she drove through these small neighborhoods, she thought about why she never settled. She enjoyed a successful career that spanned fifteen years, living in half a dozen postings around the country and some overseas assignments, but had little to show for it. Zeke Cabot had never put down roots anywhere. She never bought a home, a car, or any permanency. The once exciting gypsy life appealed to her adventurous side and soon it became a life-style of challenges and opportunities for advancement. Now, at thirty-nine, it all seemed so pointless. When she wasn't absorbed with her job, Zeke felt like an outsider looking in through the windows into what most people routinely enjoyed—hearth and home.

She blinked back the threatening sadness. The contradictions in her life, especially the recent tragic accidents, made her aware of her own mortality, her loneliness. Those weeks in the company of a beautiful and caring woman chipped away at the wall Zeke had erected to protect herself.

She parked the rental car on the street in front of the small one story two-bedroom home. Zeke pocketed the keys of her rental car. *I could probably buy a house like this and pay cash. Why haven't I done it?* Her memory flicked again to the wonderful home in New Mexico and the alluring woman waiting for her. "I wonder what it would be like to be driving home to a 'house' after working all day, instead of going to another hotel." She smiled at the glowing porch lights awaiting her.

T.J. opened the door, greeted her with a bear hug. "How's my second favorite girl in the whole world?"

Zeke laughed for the first time in days. "I'm good, but second best—really?"

"C'mon in and relax. We got some catching up to do."

T.J. took the offered wine bottle, walked over, and set it on the kitchen counter while Zeke hung her jacket on a peg by the door.

Zeke smiled as she looked around the comfortable living room, small dining room, and adjacent kitchen. Soft muted colors adorned the walls and furniture and showed off Cheryl's decorating skills. A large trophy case in one corner displayed T. J.'s collection of athletic awards.

"Hi, Zeke, welcome. I'll be right out." Cheryl's voice came from the kitchen along with an intoxicating aroma.

Zeke's jaw dropped. "She's not fixing—"

"Yes she is. Home style fried chicken, mashed potatoes, corn bread, and fresh green beans, just for you."

"I can't believe it. That's a wonderful surprise. I might have to kick you to the curb for your woman."

"Not so fast, missy, I got her first. *You* were the also-ran."

Cheryl joined them. "What're you two up to? Teej, what kind of host are you? You haven't even poured the wine. Hi, Zeke, darlin', it's so good to see you again." Cheryl pulled Zeke into a very warm embrace then held her at arm's length. "You're lookin' fine, put on a little weight, and got some color on that gorgeous face." She stroked Zeke's face.

Zeke always loved Cheryl's protective, nurturing personality. And Cheryl was, by far, the best cook she'd met other than her grandmother. Short and voluptuous, Cheryl exuded sex appeal. "I'm glad to see you too, Cheryl. You are still the sexiest woman alive." Zeke kissed her cheek.

T.J. poured and served everyone wine after they all sat down.

Zeke held up her glass. "To my oldest and dearest friends."

"T.J. tells me that you have actually found somebody worth dating. Got pictures?" Cheryl winked.

"Wait. Yes, I do." Zeke fished out her cell phone and found a nice shot of Anne in Taos with the late afternoon sun grazing her glowing skin and hair. Even in a small cell phone picture, her eyes twinkled with life.

"Oh, Zeke, she's beautiful," Cheryl said.

"Hey, I wanna see." T.J. reached over, and her partner handed her the phone. "Hot damn. You never said how smoldering hot this chick was."

"Of course, I didn't. I know you better than that. I didn't want constant crap talk from you about my love life."

T.J. turned to Cheryl. "Did I just hear right? Did Zeke Cabot just use the word 'love' in a sentence?"

"Believe you did. Should I call a doctor? Do you think it's that smack in the head she got?"

"All right you two, are you gonna feed me or sit around and abuse me all night?"

"Dunno, babe, what would you like to do?" T.J. asked Cheryl.

"Teasing Zeke is always fun, but I did slave over this meal. Maybe we could do both."

†

After dinner, Cheryl left the two friends to clean up the kitchen, while she went to her ASPCA meeting. It gave them a chance to talk a little more freely. The task took long enough for T.J. to prod Zeke about the budding romance. Once they finished they adjourned to the living room. Another glass of wine with dinner, T.J.'s persistence, and the comfortable couch loosened Zeke's internal Kevlar protection.

"Yes, Anne's very special," Zeke admitted. Those few weeks in New Mexico with an alluring and compassionate woman had softened the raw, bruised agent. When she described everything to her oldest friend, for the first time, it validated the tender new feelings, and reinforced her desire to build a relationship with Anne.

"I'm thrilled for you, Z, really. You deserve a little sunshine in your life. So tell me why you're here and she's there?"

"Like I told you, Hartbrooke asked me to come back to wrap-up some loose ends from the last case."

"Okay. And, she couldn't come with you? Must've been hard to leave her. You know, we'd love to meet her and y'all could have stayed here."

Zeke stood up suddenly and went out to the kitchen. A knot tightened in her stomach. She hadn't told T.J. about her attack. The painful memories and humiliation stung like an open sore. She returned with two bottles of water from the refrigerator, handed a bottle to T.J. before walking over to the trophy case.

"Fuck." Zeke clenched the plastic bottle in her hand and twisted the cap even tighter. Perspiration beaded on her forehead. "I don't want to do this but I have to try."

"Try what, Zeke? You're creepin' me out a little, here."

The room felt small and airless. Zeke rolled her shoulders and took a deep breath. Her chest ached and she wanted to scream. She closed her eyes briefly and then started. "There's another reason I had to leave and it's really hard to talk about." Her heart was pounding in her chest and she couldn't take a deep breath. "Anne and I had a really awful experience and—it was my fault."

T. J.'s tall frame perched on the edge of the couch. "Jesus, Zeke, why didn't you tell me? I would have come out there in a heartbeat."

"I know you would. We're both okay, but it really messed me up badly. You know that protective wall that keeps people out, went up instantly." Zeke sat uncomfortably on the arm of the chair across from T.J. "It happened right after our first night together. It was the first time in years that I allowed somebody to get that close. I convinced myself that I might actually have a chance at a relationship."

There was silence.

"Tell me, Z."

T.J. got up, retrieved the wine bottle, and poured them both another glass.

Zeke gave an abbreviated version of the surprise attack at Columbine Creek campground. She sat with her elbows resting on her knees while she stared at the pattern in the carpet. She admitted that they caught her off guard. Some asshole held a loaded gun to her girlfriend's head while another dirt bag kid, smashed Zeke's face, ripped her clothes, and attempted to rape her.

"Holy fucking shit." T.J. hissed. "Bastards. He...he raped you?"

"He didn't succeed because Anne pulled him off of me. I guess. I was unconscious."

"Did they catch 'em?"

"They have them ID'd. Maybe they have by now— I don't know. All I know is, whenever I look at Anne's beautiful face and think about the terror in her eyes, I want to kill somebody."

Zeke gulped the last of the wine in her glass and stood up. "T.J., I'm trained better than that. It should never have happened. It was my fault. I can't risk ever putting her in harm's way." The cracks deep in her soul were starting to widen. "I'm pretty fucked up, T.J.. I care more about her, than I ever dreamed I could. I would gladly give my life for her, but I can't risk hers. Do you understand?" Tears burned down Zeke's face and she heard the agonized cry from her throat.

T.J. moved quickly, pulled her best friend into her arms, and held her tightly. "Let it go, baby, let it all go."

Zeke clung to her friend and struggled to contain the grief, rage, and torment that roiled inside her soul. Hot tears ran freely down her face and her body shook with sobs of anguish.

T.J. finally pulled back a little and reached for a handful of tissue. "You know I'm here for you...always. But, babe, you're hurting inside and you have to get some help. You can't keep tryin' to do this on your own. It ain't workin', darlin'."

"I know." Zeke's wave of grief and shame subsided.

T.J. stroked Zeke's hair and held her face in both hands. "Promise you'll talk to that doctor while you're here and take the meds if you have to, Zeke. You have to get better. This isn't you, and you've got someone special waiting for you. Please, promise me?"

"I will, tomorrow. Do you think we could keep this between us?" Zeke wiped her face.

"You bet, buddy."

†

Zeke struggled under a heavy weight from which she tried to escape. Her arms and legs refused to obey and her eyes were dry and scratchy. The popcorn ceiling told her she was back in the motel. Evidently, she had fallen asleep and hadn't moved a muscle all night. Good news at least she had slept. The emotional catharsis exhausted her enough to provide several hours of uninterrupted sleep.

She managed to roll onto her side and squint one eye at the clock radio. Eight-fifteen—she didn't need to hurry since the first scheduled meeting began at ten. Zeke pulled the covers up around her neck and smiled. The evening away from work with her friends was both enjoyable and apparently therapeutic. Laughing, crying, and drinking too much wine siphoned off her excess nervous energy.

Coffee and a hot shower cleared the cobwebs sufficiently. Morning brought new clarity. Zeke booted up her computer and searched for the phone number of the psychiatrist she had seen before starting her time off. Outside the window, the sounds of rush hour traffic provided a loud reminder that she was back in the city.

"Yes, my name is, Zeke Cabot and I saw Dr. Nilsson a couple of months ago. I'm in Chicago for a few days and I was wondering if she had any time available today."

The receptionist put her on hold and the background Muzak sounded like a Beethoven symphony, which, reminded her of college days. Her first roommate, a girl from New Orleans, was a music major. Over the course of two years, simply by listening to her roommate's assignments, Zeke learned a lot about the classics. She still enjoyed Beethoven. *I'll bet this is one of his early pieces.*

"Yes, I'm here. Really? That would be terrific. I'll be there."

When her Chicago undercover assignment had concluded several weeks earlier, the neurologist she had been seeing referred her to a psychiatrist. Dr. Nilsson specialized in posttraumatic stress disorder. The neurologist from the hospital apparently thought that the grotesque decapitation homicides—especially the last one, of her friend Dr. Shayla Graham, could have delayed effects on the undercover agent.

Zeke was loath to admit it, but the man was right, she had no idea the delayed symptoms were so powerful. *Odd.* Just by talking to T.J., and making an appointment with Dr. Nilsson, brought her a little relief. Although she was tired, the coiled spring in her chest had relaxed.

A dark turtleneck with charcoal slacks seemed appropriate. She folded the cuffs of the cashmere turtleneck, and removed a narrow black belt from her carry-on bag and threaded it through the belt loops as she made a mental list. Zeke attached her badge and holster before picking up her duty weapon from the bedside table. After double-checking the magazine for the Glock 22, she slid it into the holster, shoved a laptop into her briefcase, and headed out for some breakfast.

Zeke had a meeting with Hartbrooke, an appointment with Dr. Nilsson, and hopefully, after that, she'd be finished with her Chicago business.

Chapter Two

Anne stood at the kitchen sink trying to match the broken pieces of the small ceramic plate. It had slipped out of her grasp as she was dusting and even though it wasn't an expensive heirloom, it held sentimental value. It was a souvenir dish her mother had bought her on a trip to Washington, DC her sophomore year. The Girl's Club trip was a reward for magazine sales and her mother was one of four chaperones. Anne smiled as she recalled the excitement of her first trip to Washington. Her mother had been so proud of her and picked out the small plate of the Lincoln Memorial because Anne had admired it.

She held two of the pieces together as the super glue dried. What had happened to that close relationship? It was easy to blame it on the drinking, but when did they really grow apart? Anne could scarcely remember now. Her mother's erratic behavior and late night phone calls had become a source of irritation and embarrassment.

After the glue set, she stared at the broken plate and a wave of guilt washed over her. In spite of it all, she loved her mother and knew that the intolerant and odd behavior of her mother drove the final wedge between them. She looked at the other items on the shelf; the flawed plate would be a daily reminder of her broken relationship. Anne forced back a wave of sadness as she turned her back and returned to the kitchen.

†

"Gosh, I feel like we haven't talked in ages, I'm glad you could visit." Susan poured fresh coffee in two handmade mugs on the cluttered kitchen counter in her kitchen.

"I don't know where the time goes. With work and everything else, I hardly have time to socialize." Anne placed a small piece of coffee cake on the plate in front of her. It was still warm and the smell of cinnamon permeated the kitchen. "This smells divine."

Her friend and neighbor, Susan Godfrey, baked perfectly wonderful delicacies.

"Jim took the boys hunting or it wouldn't have lasted this long." She shook her head. "I'm glad they got the chance to hunt with their dad. They deserve a little male bonding time. The upside for me—I have a few days where I'm not picking up after three men." She carried the cups to the table. "How are things at your house?" A wicked grin accompanied her raised eyebrows.

Anne laughed. "Things are just fine, thank you. And yes, before you say anything, I asked Zeke to move in with me."

"Honey, you know I would never intrude in your business."

"The heck you wouldn't. I'm surprised you haven't bought a telescope," said Anne, only half jokingly.

"How do you know I haven't? You haven't been up to the third floor lately." Susan barely contained her laugh. "I just want you to be happy, honey." She reached over to squeeze Anne's arm.

"Thanks." She paused and sipped the flavorful coffee. "You know, I am happy. I wouldn't have believed it six months ago, but I feel younger, more vibrant. And when we're together, it's—it's hard to describe. I feel like I must be glowing. Honestly, Susan, I wasn't sure I would ever be able to love anyone again after the way Andrew betrayed me. You know, I really believed he and I were soul mates destined to be together forever."

"I know, I thought Andrew was perfect too. You were a beautiful couple. It just wasn't meant to be. The fact is you do look much happier."

The familiar flutter started in Anne's chest. "I feel like a high school girl with her first crush. I think about her all day and dream about her at night." she stopped. Her face flushed and she realized how crazy it all sounded. She looked across at Susan's kind but quizzical expression then sipped some coffee, clasping the cup with both hands. "I'm sorry to sound so goofy. This mysterious woman has captivated my heart as no one ever has. I feel a little silly talking this way, I mean, it sounds so adolescent." Anne could feel the warmth spread.

Susan put her empty cup down. "Why didn't you bring her over? I would love to meet her."

"Well, she was recalled to Chicago for some work related business."

"How come you didn't go with her?"

"Good question. She didn't ask and neither did I. But I'm wondering if she isn't having second thoughts."

"Why on earth would you say a thing like that? I thought this woman would move heaven and earth for you. Surely she wouldn't let a wonderful woman like you get away."

"I honestly don't know. When I say she's mysterious, it's because she is. I mean, she keeps her life pretty compartmentalized and I think it will take a long time for her to open up completely—if ever."

Susan refilled their coffee cups.

Anne continued, "Sometimes I feel as though we've known each other forever, you know, like in the past life or something. Then, in a heartbeat, she'll change before my eyes and become someone I hardly recognize."

"It sounds like you're pretty serious about this woman. Do you have any second thoughts about it being a lesbian relationship?"

Anne sat up a little straighter and looked at her friend. "I think about that a lot." It was true. After Zeke had left, Anne found herself watching people at work, on the street, or wherever she went, she watched women. Every time she saw two women together, she wondered if they were 'together' and how difficult was it for them?

Several of her co-workers were openly gay and her employer offered insurance for partners. It wasn't like she was unfamiliar. There was little doubt that her mother would either ignore it or be entirely dismissive. It didn't much matter. She had no other family or close friends other than Susan, who'd talk about it with her, so it really rested with her own conscience.

The alternative was unbearable. Zeke Cabot made her happier than she'd been in years.

"I want this to work and I'm going to do whatever I have to do." Anne said somewhat defiantly.

"When will she be back?"

"I'm not really sure, she said a few days." Anne continued to push crumbs around her plate. In quiet moments, worry nibbled at her happiness. The short amount of time they had been apart brought their budding relationship clearly into focus. She no longer doubted that Zeke Cabot had captured her heart completely. The question kept rattling around her head. Were those feelings mutual?

The accidental and coincidental meetings threw them together quickly. One gloriously romantic night together in a Taos inn melded them together followed the next day by a freakish attack, which loosened the bond they were forming. Then Zeke left. She claimed she had to go and it was clear at that point that her career as a special agent took precedence over everything—including Anne.

"Don't fret about it too much. If this woman is as special as you say she is, give her a little time. You've waited to find someone new; don't throw in the towel yet," Susan said. The phone rang. "Excuse me a minute, hon."

Anne leaned back and looked out Susan's patio door. Her own house was just barely visible through the pine trees. She walked around the table, folded her arms close to her, and closed her eyes. With no effort, Zeke's lovely face and gold-flecked brown eyes appeared. The small tingling sensation began in the middle of her chest and spread through her like a warm wave. It took little for Anne to recreate the warm sensations of soft kisses and warm embraces. From there it was only a short step to the heightened sense of arousal and yearning.

"I'm so sorry, that was Jim. One of the boys got hurt, and they're on their way to Saint Vincent's in Santa Fe. I told him I'd meet them there."

"Is it anything serious?"

"No, I don't think so. He fell and hurt his leg. Jim just wants to check it out."

"Well, call me when you get back." Anne pulled on her jacket.

Susan walked her to the door and gave her a quick embrace. "I will. You take care of yourself."

✝

Anne walked around the side of the house and cut through the woods to get to her property. Most of the leaves had fallen by this time of the year except for a few sturdy oaks that would hold on through the winter. Sunlight dappled the ground as it peeked through the branches.

It reminded her of cool dry fall days in the Midwest. Anne kicked through the deep blanket of leaves inhaling the rich loamy smell. She hugged her jacket a little tighter and took a deep breath. She loved autumn with the rich colors and smells. It was a time of year when she began to hibernate, in preparation for winter and seclusion.

The past two years had been an adjustment and she discovered that living alone after her painful and humiliating divorce was not all bad. She had her books and lately had been reading up on photography. Although the horses took a good deal of her time, Anne enjoyed studying new interests.

A brightly colored leaf caught her attention and she bent over to pick it up, smiling. The golden-flecked leaf reminded her once again of the reflective glitter that first caught her attention when she saw Zeke's cat-like brown eyes. She rubbed the leaf with her thumb and allowed herself to daydream about living with the woman whose magical touch she could remember vividly. A tiny shiver shot up her spine.

Outside of her family, the only woman she had ever lived with was a roommate in nursing school. After a few minor skirmishes, which she now realized was quite normal; she and Kate had become good friends. Still, living with Zeke would be an entirely different experience. Kate had been a loyal friend and they shared many good experiences and more than a few bad.

Zeke, on the other hand, shared very little. And yet, the chemistry and the physical attraction were so overpowering that Anne experienced actual withdrawal symptoms when she was apart from Zeke. "That's ridiculous. I can't believe I'm admitting that, even to myself."

Anne hurried through her back door to catch the ringing phone. "Hello?" No response. The caller ID showed it was a call from the Benevolent Order of Police. "That's the third solicitation call this month. Why couldn't it just be my benevolent federal agent?" Anne hung her jacket in the mudroom after shutting the backdoor.

She sighed looking around her tidy, ordered kitchen. Whenever life overran its banks, she started an O.C.—organization crusade. With Zeke gone, her energy focused on the kitchen. It hadn't looked this good since the epic divorce O.C. She glanced at the snapshots on the refrigerator door. A few of the pictures were from the trip to Taos. Her favorite was a picture of Zeke leaning against a lodgepole pine near Red River. Rays of low angle light from the early morning sun highlighted a lock of hair on her forehead along with the right side of her face. She squinted and offered just the hint of a smile. Anne reached out and ran her finger down side of the print. "Where are you Zeke Cabot?"

†

"I think that should just about do it." Special Agent in Charge Frank Hartbrooke closed the file folder and laid both hands on top. "I appreciate you interrupting your vacation to finish this up, but I can't say that I really understand it all yet. The financial misdirection will take some time to unravel. The Hussein brothers were involved in a lot more than the initial homicide investigation revealed." He pinched the bridge of his nose and leaned his head back.

Zeke knew he wasn't finished.

"I think I'll pass this off to white collar crimes and let them sort it out. The U.S. Attorney is still arguing with Justice about getting Ahmed Hussein to stand trial in Chicago. Maybe this new information will help. Anyway, I'm sorry about that nasty incident in New Mexico but the two men who did this should be locked up soon and will be prosecuted. You have my word."

"Thank you, sir, that's good to know. At least I won't have to be looking over my shoulder for the next few weeks." Zeke sighed and peeked at her watch. The appointment with Dr. Nilsson in forty minutes was across town.

"I'll review this," he indicated the white envelope Zeke had handed him when they started, "and let you know." He tossed it in his in-box and then he leaned forward on his elbows, with his chin propped on his fist. "Are you finished here in Chicago and ready to head back to the mountains?"

Zeke swallowed hard. At that moment, she knew that he was concerned about the recent assault. They both knew. "Well, not quite. I thought I'd talk to Dr. Nilsson this afternoon. In fact, I have an appointment." Zeke squirmed in her chair and clenched her hands together under the overhang of his desk. "I—I thought I should talk to her about—well, about the attack."

He gave a small nod. "I think that's probably a good idea. On top of everything else, you didn't need another 'incident' to deal with."

When he looked at her, Zeke could see the sadness in his eyes.

"I am sorry. I'm not going to insult you by telling you I know what you're going through because I don't. But I do know someone who has. Several years ago we had an agent in the L.A. Field office that had a very similar situation."

Her boss started typing on his keyboard. "Her name is Sandra Spinelli." He pulled a Post-it off and started writing. "She lives in Arizona now. I'm not sure if it'll help, but I think it would be worth a try for you to call her. At least she could tell you how she dealt with it." He reached across the desk with the yellow slip of paper. "She offered to do this if any other female agent needed help."

"Thank you." Zeke took the paper and read the name and number. She folded the note and put it in her jacket pocket. "I'll give her a call, sir."

He reached his hand out. "Good luck, Agent Cabot."

Zeke waited for the elevator thinking about Agent Hartbrooke's suggestion. *Of course, he couldn't understand. The sexual assault of FBI agents didn't occur on a regular basis.* After pushing the button for the ground floor, Zeke pulled out the Post-it and read the name again. The idea of talking to another female agent who had experienced the same indignity might be a good idea.

✝

Zeke was lucky that the midday traffic was light and she reached Dr. Nilsson's office on Michigan Avenue with five minutes to spare. When she arrived at the office, the waiting room was empty and Dr. Nilsson's door stood open.

"Hello?"

"Agent Cabot, please come in. I didn't expect to see you so soon. I thought you were enjoying some well deserved time off."

They each took a seat in one of the comfortable club chairs at a round coffee table. In the center, a teak tray held a carafe and several glasses. Natural light from several floor-to-ceiling panels provided plenty of light and the indirect recessed lights added a pleasant ambiance. Zeke tried to get comfortable—something she rarely did in any office. It was even truer when the subject of conversation would be her.

"I was, until I got the call of duty." She tried to laugh. "Actually, Agent Hartbrooke asked if I could come back to Chicago briefly to sort out some loose ends."

Dr. Nilsson was probably around sixty with silver-grey hair pulled back in a braid. She was tall, close to Zeke's nearly six foot height and slender. Zeke thought the pale skin and eyes were clearly Scandinavian features. The warm smile was disarming.

"I see." Dr. Nilsson folded her hands in her lap as she crossed her leg.

Zeke tried to relax.

"I wanted to come back, at least for a little while." Zeke shifted in her chair and shoved her hands under her legs to keep from trembling. "There was...I had...I was attacked and, sexually assaulted." *Fuck. I can't believe I just said that.* She looked at the bookcase trying to avoid the doctor's gaze. Zeke sped through a very brief summary of the attack in the campground in the mountains and subsequent hospital treatment. "Mostly it was a lot of bruising and a broken nose."

"Was that what you wanted to talk to me about?"

"Well, yes. But there's something else." She cleared her throat. "I met someone when I arrived in New Mexico and she was with me that day. Our initial meeting was kind of an accident; then we bumped into each other on three separate occasions. The last time was when I fell off a hiking trail and she, well—she kind of rescued me. Because I injured my ankle, we ended up spending a fair amount of time together and developed a strong attraction to one another." Thinking about Anne settled her. She shifted and crossed her legs. "The trip to Taos was our first weekend getaway together and it was wonderful. I never dreamt I could be so happy. Too happy. I got careless." The muscles in her abdomen tightened. "Two armed men caught us off guard. The attempted rape was unsuccessful, but ever since then, I feel...I haven't been the same."

"Can you tell me more about that?"

Zeke felt her heart thudding against her ribs. She looked up into gentle blue eyes. Dr. Nilsson wore a concerned expression with their head tilted slightly to one side.

"I really care for this woman and we were just beginning to get close, intimate. But ever since we got back to her house, I've been afraid. When she touches me, even a simple thing like a hug feels constricting, like I can't get my breath and I don't understand it."

Zeke reached for the carafe and poured water into one of the glasses. She gulped it and put the glass down seeing a telltale tremor in her right hand.

"While I was working undercover here in Chicago, I was pretty closed off emotionally. I had to be to

25

survive and it made me feel like I'd never have normal sexual desires again. When I met Anne, that's her name, feelings started to wake up. It was exciting to find out that I could still be interested and aroused." A brief flicker of light went off in her head. In that instant, she relived the incredible bliss that she had when they made love for the first time. A momentary wave of peace washed over her. "In spite of the utter joy I experienced with her, I feel like I've lost my moorings. I can't seem to connect to solid ground. Do you know what I mean?"

"I think so, but go on."

Zeke rubbed her hand across to her eyes. *Where are the words?* "Sometimes when I'm in a conversation, especially about work, I have trouble staying focused and I can't feel the floor under my feet or the chair I'm sitting in. It's like floating, a little. Focusing is difficult because I feel so spacey."

"Difficulty focusing is a very common symptom. From what you've described, Agent Cabot, your reaction seems fairly typical. Tell me, has your sleep been disturbed?"

"Not much more than it was when I left here, but some nights are better than others."

"How about your appetite?"

"That's improved some. Of course, the food is terrific out there. I just don't always think to eat."

"If you remember, when I saw you the last time, I suggested you try some medication for anxiety. I did that because I suspected your undercover assignment created acute posttraumatic stress disorder. You realize a new incident would only compound that." She uncrossed her legs and leaned forward with her arms resting on her knees.

"PTSD is unpredictable at best. There may be

Defying Gravity

times when you feel fine, and without any warning, you may notice mild symptoms, some anxiety, loss of focus, or a full-blown panic attack. There's no way to know what might trigger those symptoms. It might help to keep track of things that precipitate the symptoms." She spoke again softly. "As I said, your reaction is not unusual. It will take some time for you to begin to trust your feelings again but I think it will be easier now that you have someone you can trust. Of course, the best thing would be for you to be honest with her."

Zeke struggled to stay in the chair and listen. Her heart was pounding and her mouth was dry. She tried to slow her breathing even as her hands trembled.

"Agent Cabot, did you hear what I said?"

"Yes, ma'am."

"You're going to be all right. Medications and therapy have proven effective in most cases. I'll be happy to work with you while you're in Chicago. Exactly how long will you be here?"

"I hope to leave soon because my work is finished. I really don't want to be in Chicago for very long, it's difficult." Zeke heard her own voice slipping into the southern drawl she used whenever she was nervous.

Dr. Nilsson stood and walked over to a desk, and returned with a prescription pad. "I'm going to give you a prescription for anxiety. I know you don't like to take medication, but I think this will help." She handed Zeke the prescription. "I would also like you to talk to somebody in Albuquerque. If you're willing, I have a friend who specializes in PTSD and I will e-mail you her name and phone number. This is not something you can do by yourself, do you understand?"

"I think so."

The doctor slid back in the chair and tented her fingers. "There's more isn't there?"

"Not really. I'll get the prescription filled. I'm sure you're right, it should help." Zeke could barely wait to escape the confines of Dr. Nilsson's office. They shook hands at the door and when it closed, Zeke slumped against the wall. Ragged breathing hurt her lungs and the pounding in her chest ached. *Shit!*

†

Her hands were trembling so badly she dropped the keys when she tried to open the trunk of her rental car. Zeke folded her blazer neatly, leaned over her carry-on suitcase, and tried to focus. The start of another panic attack threatened and she didn't want anything to derail her plans. She had to get out of Chicago. Zeke pocketed the prescription and carefully put her blazer in the suitcase. She pulled on her leather jacket and slammed the trunk. Her hands rested on the cool metal as she forced slow deep breaths

More than anything, she wanted to be back in Anne's house—her safe space. She needed to be there and yearned for the comforting embrace of the woman who'd captured her reluctant heart. She felt a little guilty that she hadn't called and told Anne about her decision to make the quick trip to Arizona. Zeke needed to talk to that other agent who had survived a similar incident in order to put some of the demons to rest.

Chapter Three

After returning her rental car and checking through TSA screening, Zeke finally collapsed in an empty seat in the boarding area. She had picked up a letter from the office for the pilot when she said goodbye to the team. The letter containing an alphanumeric code that was required when carrying a loaded weapon on a plane, and she would present it to him when she boarded.

Next stop, Flagstaff, Arizona and a meeting with retired Special Agent Sandra Spinelli. She promised herself to call Anne as soon as she settled in Flagstaff.

After opening another package of antacids, she checked her phone for messages. No new calls. *I hope that means I can let go of the case and Chicago.*

Zeke had explained she was getting restless and edgy in the city when T.J. complained that her friend was leaving town too quickly. It was growing harder for Zeke to concentrate or even to sit still. She noticed that her right leg bounced whenever she sat for too long. Even T.J. had commented on it.

As badly as she wanted to get back to New Mexico, there was a stronger desire to put this last incident behind her for good. Anne deserved better, much better. She deserved a partner who could be fully present. Right now, Zeke didn't think she could provide it.

"Nonstop service to Phoenix Arizona, now boarding—"

She had been lucky to get a direct flight to Phoenix

with a connecting flight to Flagstaff on American West. Relaxing in the seat, Zeke allowed herself to go off duty for a couple of minutes. Years of experience caused her to be extra careful in public places, especially when traveling. There were easily a dozen times that day that some individual or situation raised her suspicion and wariness. What seemed like normal or even mildly eccentric behavior before 9-11 nowadays might be a lead up to an emergency. Most airport security personnel were ill equipped to handle today's threats and only briefly trained to be screening travelers. Recent studies had shown that a variety of weapons could still be smuggled onto an airplane. Zeke felt more secure with a loaded 9 mm automatic close to her side.

†

The Flagstaff Radisson Hotel was elegant and her room was huge, with a king sized Sleep Number Bed on which she flopped as soon as the bellhop left. *Man I wish Annie was here.* Zeke stretched her arms and legs while conjuring the memorable tryst in Taos in the candle lit suite with the sunken tub. In her memory, that night had been the most romantic of her life. The chemistry and the sexual tension had been powerful aphrodisiacs. Zeke had waited patiently to be certain that Anne shared the same intense feelings. And as a result, they shared an exquisite experience on which to build a relationship.

All of the passion and all of the chemistry would be for nothing if Zeke couldn't get a grip on her fragile and damaged psyche. She lay still and felt the ache of desire grow.

†

It was eight p.m. when Anne picked up the phone in her kitchen.

"Hi Annie, what're you doing right now?"

Anne laughed at hearing her lover's voice. "Making love to the cabana boy—why?"

"Because I had an idea. Do you work tomorrow?"

"Yes."

"Well, can you meet me in Flagstaff tomorrow night?" Zeke asked.

Anne's heart skipped a beat, her pulse quickened, and then the logistical planning began—horses, house, charting, check. Plans? None. She started scribbling notes on the pad by the phone. "What are you doing in Flagstaff and why would I come over there when you're so close?"

"I have to meet with a local special agent tomorrow and this is a great hotel with an enormous king sized bed—I'm afraid I'll be lonely. Plus, the Grand Canyon is close by, so I thought we could do some sightseeing. You know, just a little getaway."

Zeke sounded so much better, how could she possibly refuse? "Let me do some checking and I'll call you back in a little while."

Anne hung up the phone as a smile emerged along with some other pleasant sensations.

†

Room service was quick and Zeke enjoyed a crisp Cobb salad while she watched CNN and flipped channels. She made a quick call to confirm the meeting time with Sandra Spinelli and then untucked her shirt, slipped off her slacks, and began to unpack.

31

In the corner of her brief case, she spotted her camera. Zeke forgot it was in there and all of the pictures they had taken on the trip to Taos. "Damn." She scrolled through the digital pictures and smiled, laughed, and blushed.

Anne had taken some provocative pictures and Zeke found herself blushing at some 'R' rated shots from their hotel room. For a divorced straight woman, this gal was seriously hot and extremely seductive. The idea of waiting twenty-four hours to see her and reacquaint herself with that voluptuous body seemed like an eternity.

Zeke lay on her back, with the camera clutched to her chest and closed her eyes. The first thing that had attracted her to Anne was the pale blond hair caught by a gentle breeze. When Anne turned to her, pale, sapphire-blue eyes captured her attention. "Oh, Annie."

Zeke's fingers tingled remembering the first touch, feel of the smooth soft skin of Anne's face, the taste of her lips, and the memory of Anne's delicate trembling fingers unbuttoning her shirt on that magical night. When Anne's palm had rested lightly on her breast, the electric jolt touched every nerve. Zeke could feel the pulse in her neck and her breathing deepened. Her desire for that touch became excruciating.

The phone interrupted her thoughts.

"I'll be able to catch a commuter flight at seven thirty p.m. that would land at eight twenty. Can you arrange for the hotel to pick me up?"Anne said.

"Sure thing."

"What should I bring to wear?"

"Nothing. You're going to be naked for forty-eight hours."

Chapter Four

At precisely nine a.m., the front desk called to announce a guest. When Zeke checked in at the Radisson the night before, Zeke had left instructions about the guest that would be visiting her. "God, I love the dependability of Agents." A few moments later, there was a knock on the door.

Zeke greeted her guest with a handshake and ushered her over to a seating area by the window with a table and two chairs. "Thank you for agreeing to meet with me. I'm sure this isn't the way you planned to spend your day."

Sandra Spinelli looked to be fiftyish, maybe five-five, grey hair, and a comfortable, retired figure lacking the rigid on duty posture of so many agents. Her alert brown eyes glimmered behind some lightly tinted frameless glasses. She wasn't wearing a wedding ring and there was a linear scar along the left side of her face.

Sandra chuckled. "No, not my normal day, but I am glad you called. I should tell you that your reputation has preceded you. I still have friends in the agency, and your name has come up on several occasions—in a good way."

"That's a little surprising, but good to know."

"Do you mind if I take the seat with the back to the window? Sometimes the glare bothers my eyes," Former agent Spinelli said.

"No of course not, I'll pull the curtains a bit. Have you eaten yet?" asked Zeke. "I was going to order something."

"Maybe some coffee and a roll."

They spent a comfortable hour or so exchanging war stories on who's who at the bureau, which offices they'd both served at, and the plight of women in service all while sipping coffee and munching on pastries. They had a few similar acquaintances and similar training stories.

Sandra had a quick wit and a wonderful laugh. Soon Zeke relaxed, she knew she'd made a good decision in coming to Flagstaff.

Finally, Sandra broke the ice. "Would it be easier if I told you my story first?"

Zeke felt her heart skip and then her pulse quickened. "Yeah, I think it might be, if you don't mind." It must've been obvious that she had been stalling.

Sandra refilled their coffee cups and leaned back in her chair while she rearranged the plate, knife, and napkin in front of her. Evidently reliving her painful experience, even after many years, made her uncomfortable.

"I was assigned to the gang unit in El Segundo, California in 2002." She took a deep breath, squared her shoulders, and looked at Zeke. "My partner and I had been looking for a small group of gangbangers terrorizing an older neighborhood. You know the stuff—breaking and entering, fights, car thefts, and armed robberies. We got a tip about a small warehouse on the east side of town and we surveilled it for about a month. It seemed to be more of a meeting place than a regular site and we were able to identify six regulars who visited.

"One morning we waited to see if we could nab a couple of them for interrogation. When we were certain that at least two of them were inside, we entered from two different doors. There were two guys doin' crack and completely unaware. When my partner announced "FBI", one guy jumped through the window and my partner went after him. I put the other kid on the floor and was ready to cuff him when someone clobbered me from behind. I was out cold." Sandra was breathing deeper and she seemed to be choosing her words carefully.

Zeke knew the story was difficult to tell, but there was nothing she could do to help.

"I woke up in another abandoned house tied to a chair and gagged. My head was throbbing and there was blood on my shirt. I didn't know whose it was. I don't mind telling you I was scared shitless. After a while, the door opened and four Hispanic toughs swaggered in—none of them looked even twenty— kids, you know. There was a lot of posturing and tough talk about how they were so much smarter than this 'FBI Bitch' and how they were gonna teach the 'chucha' a lesson for messing with their bad asses."

Zeke's pulse quickened and felt her rising blood pressure pulsing in her temples as her fingers curled into a fist. Her recent memories clawed at her, pulling her back.

Sandra took a sip of coffee; the cup vibrated in her hands as she continued. "They took turns punching and threatening me and then one of them ripped my shirt while a second one slashed at my face. The sight of the blood must have set them off like a pack of hungry sharks because they yanked me out of the chair while they ripped at my clothes." Her voice cracked.

Sandra's face lost most of its color and she held tight to the arms of the chair. "They took turns, one after the other until I wished they had killed me. I must have passed out because I don't remember anything until the sound of crashing glass and wood. A dozen agents and cops stormed the place. Apparently, a neighbor called after hearing the noise."

Sandra sat up, picked up her cup from the table, and looked Zeke in the eye. "They were all convicted after a long trial and sent to North Kern."

Both agents sat in silence for several minutes.

"I know it's a little early but would you like a drink, because I sure would," said Zeke.

"Sounds good," Sandra nodded.

Zeke brought over several small bottles—whisky, rum, bourbon, and brandy from the minibar. "Pick your poison"

They each selected one and poured it into the now empty coffee cups.

The assault and attempted rape, although very recent, seemed somehow less horrific compared to Sandra's story. It was still raw nevertheless.

Zeke finally broke the silence. "Okay, I guess it's my turn." She decided to abbreviate part of the story and started when they reached the Columbine Creek campground. She detailed their questioning and attempted rape at gunpoint. When she finished her face glistened with perspiration that dampened her chest as her leg bounced. She drained the small amount of whisky remaining in her coffee.

Sandra just shook her head. "Wow, I am so sorry. Fucking bastards. Was your friend okay?"

"Yeah, she got cuts and bruises but I think she did more damage to the attacker." Zeke remembered Anne telling her about punching and kicking the inept assailant.

"Did they catch the guys?" Sandra unscrewed the cap from the small bottle of scotch.

Zeke thought about Frank Hartbrooke's promise. He told her that they had an ID and were getting ready for an arrest. "Not yet, but they will."

"Believe it or not, for me, knowing those guys are locked helps. It didn't undo anything, but at least I didn't have to look over my shoulder anymore."

Zeke leaned forward. "Sandra, how did the attack affect you—you know, professionally and personally?"

"I suppose that's the million dollar question isn't it." She leaned forward with her forearms resting on the table, her fingers rotating the coffee cup in front of her. "I was in the hospital for about a week. I had several broken bones and some infected lacerations on my legs, one in my face, as well as a concussion. Eventually they let my husband take me home.

"It took awhile, at least six months before I was cleared for light-duty. My partner had asked for reassignment because he felt guilty about the whole thing. It wasn't his fault, but I couldn't convince him of that. You know losing my partner was almost as bad. So, I worked the desk for a long time because I wasn't up to the job physically or emotionally. It was hard at the office because everyone knew what happened."

Zeke watched as the woman's strong composure slipped into a blanket of sadness.

"My husband—he couldn't deal with it and divorced me. I was damaged goods and he couldn't understand how a trained law enforcement profession could 'let that happen'". Sandra turned her head to the window and Zeke watched her face as the muscles tightened in her jaw. She swiped at her eyes with a closed fist and then picked up her coffee cup.

"Once in a while, I have a nightmare or see someone on the street that reminds me, but for the most part, I'm okay and I manage pretty well. I get that it wasn't my fault—there was nothing my partner or I could have done differently. Still, it was the end of a career that I loved."

Zeke shook her head and looked at the brave woman who had shared a very personal part of her life. "Sandra, I really appreciate you sharing your story. Man, you've been through hell. Has the bureau been there for you, I mean, do you feel supported?"

"For the most part, yes. All the treatment was covered. But it didn't take long to realize that it was a dirty little secret that no one wanted to talk about. That's why I eventually left and took disability."

Zeke nodded. "That's what I worry about. I think I can get back in shape and be able to function, but this whole ordeal has created, I don't know—a crisis of confidence. I feel like I'm always second guessing myself and feeling unsure. That has never been a problem—believe me. I have always been quick and very decisive. I've lost something and I need some help."

Sandra nodded. "Don't get too stressed, that'll all come back. Besides, there are a lot more resources today than when I got hurt. As soon as you get back to work, you'll start using your skills. Remember, Zeke, you are a highly trained professional. Your reflexes alone will carry you in almost every case, just don't over think."

"I have to believe you, because you've done it."

"But…" Sandra cocked her head.

"Well, there is something else." Zeke took a deep breath. She then briefly shared how she had met Anne and developed a strong attraction that 'may' have clouded her 'highly trained' mind.

Sandra laughed at the comment and broke the tension. "I get it, not so good for a professional but certainly understandable."

"The problem is my self-confidence issue is extending to the bedroom. I feel so closed off now. I'm not sure I can be the person that Anne was originally attracted to and it scares me. I'm afraid of losing her and I'm afraid I can't protect her." *Afraid*. She said the word aloud—afraid that she was unable to protect herself or protect her lover. Zeke stopped. An icy coldness bloomed in her chest and her throat tightened.

"I know. I know what that feels like," Sandra tenderly said.

Zeke began to cry softly and she covered her face with her hands. She had named the demon.

Sandra went to the bathroom and retrieved a handful of tissues, handed them to Zeke, then poured them each another drink.

"Zeke, you have to remember something important, you are the same woman that you were a month ago or six months ago. You're smart, you're capable, and you're beautiful—inside and out. Whatever happened to you in that clearing was just a bad thing. It was like breaking your leg or having your house burn down. It's a horrible fact—but it does not define 'you'. Any 'emotional baggage' is something you have attached to it. Any meaning is a meaning that *you* created in your head—it's not real."

Sandra moved her chair a little closer and grasped Zeke's wrist. "Human beings want everything to 'mean' something and we make up meanings to rationalize our reactions. Believe me, I know. You got hurt. But, you decided to make it mean that you made a mistake and therefore you are worthless. Shit. Does that sound logical to you?"

Zeke was somewhat stunned by Sandra's 'tough love', but had to admit it made some sense.

They continued a little longer until the conversation turned to more mundane topics that lightened the mood. By four p.m. Zeke stood up, thoroughly drained. "I think we deserve a special dinner. My treat."

The Thursday special in the hotel dining room was prime rib, which explained the crowd. Zeke's last minute call for reservation netted them a small table near the window.

"I can't thank you enough for coming over here and providing a day of therapy. I feel much better unloading this burden with someone who's actually had a similar experience. There are only so many times I can listen to the damn platitudes, 'that must be awful', or 'I can't imagine how you feel'."

"You're right, I still get those—along with the sympathetic stares. Listen, I'm glad I could help and you know it helped me too. Even though it was a long time ago, I think sharing the experience has helped me feel less alone. And, I'm glad I got to meet you, Zeke Cabot. What are your plans now?"

Zeke smiled. "Well, I actually called my lady and asked her to meet me here for a couple of days. I thought we could see the Grand Canyon. We need to have some serious discussions before we settle into an actual relationship with a daily routine."

"Sounds like good plan. I'd love to meet the lucky girl. If you want, maybe we could have dinner one night?"

"That would be great."

They parted as friends with a warm embrace and renewed strength.

†

Impatient, Zeke started calling the front desk around seven-thirty to be sure that the courtesy car would be available to pick up Ms. Reynolds. She changed clothes twice and paced the floor alternately turning the TV on then off. Her mind was racing with a million thoughts about Anne, Sandra's words, her job, a future with a real partner, and most of all hers fears.

She cast one more critical look in the mirror to be sure she looked casual, but sharp. *Shirt tails in or out?* Studying this important element of her wardrobe, she quickly tucked them in. After a forced smile, Zeke hurried to the bathroom and brushed her teeth again. Hell, would Anne even want to kiss her?

When she went back to Chicago, it was to get better. She had promised Anne to get the demons under control before returning. *I want to feel whole and complete—not like damaged goods. Not as a broken vessel but a woman completely ready to give and receive, love.*

Was she ready? More than anything, she wanted to feel that fire in her belly and the passion it produced. As it was, what she felt chilled more than warmed her. Even her view of the multicolored evening sky through the window, while spectacular, provided no answers. She remained conflicted by her dueling thoughts and feelings. Pacing didn't help.

This uncertainty was new and uncomfortable. Her military father instilled self-confidence and decisiveness throughout her life. It was those qualities and her athleticism that earned her a reputation as a top-notch federal agent.

Zeke pulled out a chair and sat down at the table near the window. The same table over which she and Sandra had shared their most humiliating and painful experiences. Somehow, it was easier to talk to Sandra rather than a therapist. Zeke leaned back and clasped her fingers behind her head. Maybe it was interacting with strangers, too many years of dealing with criminals, or too many years of hardened distrust that jaded her. Or, way too many years of living alone and watching over her shoulder every single day. The job had taken a toll that she hadn't even noticed until now.

Even when she tried, it was hard to remember when the unraveling began, sometime during her assignment in Chicago, after going to the crime scene of her first victim from the serial killer. The memory of those decapitated homeless victims caused an icy ripple down her spine. *Was that when it started? Or was it after the concussion from the car accident?* She rubbed her arms from the imaginary chill.

The past month passed in a blur. One event landed on the next and then harder on the next until all of them were cascading like broken dominoes layered with screams.

She scrubbed her face with her palms and stood up. "Okay, the past is the past. It's time I put it all behind me. Because dammit, for the first time in a long time, I have hope and a chance to be loved."

On impulse, Zeke snatched up her cell phone, paused, and dialed a familiar number.

"Hello?" Comfort.

"Hi, Mom, it's me."

"Zari, is it really you, honey? Oh, I'm so glad you called. You know everyone asks about you. I just tell them that you'll be home from school soon. How're you doing?"

Zeke's throat tightened. "I'm fine, Mom. I'm in Arizona right now and I'm going to see the Grand Canyon. How are you and Dad?"

"We're fine, honey, don't you worry. I sure miss

you. Your Dad's here, do you want to talk with him? Robert, it's Zari on the phone, come talk to her."

Zeke corrected her posture in anticipation and listened while her mother juggled the phone, muttering.

"To what do we owe this honor or is something wrong?" Her father's deep baritone voice resonated.

"Nothing's wrong, sir, I just wanted to check and see how you and Mom were doing?"

"We just got home from dinner with your brother and his family. It's always wonderful to see them and that little girl is just the apple of his eye. Beautiful child, I'm very proud of them."

"I'm sorry I missed them when I was there, but he has sent me some pictures." There was an uncomfortable pause and Zeke paced a little faster. "Dad, how is Mom doing? She seems really forgetful tonight. Has she been to the doctor yet?"

"Your mother's a little tired tonight, that's all. She's been terribly busy this week with her clubs and the fall bake sale. She's always much sharper in the morning, so we try to go to bed a little earlier."

"I'm just worried. You know her blood pressure has always been a little unpredictable and that's why grandpa had a stroke."

"I appreciate your concern, but I'm keeping an eye on your mother, as I always have. So are you still on vacation?"

Zeke wilted. That conversation was over. "Yes, sir. I needed to make a stop in Arizona but I'll be heading back to New Mexico. I asked for a transfer to Albuquerque. It's really beautiful out here and much less stressful."

"Well, if that's your choice. Not sure if there's much chance for advancement. Too bad you couldn't be reassigned back to Washington."

The same old discussion. "Maybe next assignment. You know, there are two important National Labs in New Mexico, as well as Kirtland Air Force base. Didn't you spend some time at Kirtland?" She knew it was probably pointless to try to engage him, but she always tried.

"Zarathustra, you have chosen your profession and I believe you will make the choices you think most appropriate."

"Yes, sir. I won't keep you, please say goodnight to Mom for me."

"I will, and you know how much your mother appreciates your calls. Good night."

"Dad…"

"Yes"

"I…take care of yourself."

"Will do. You do the same."

Zeke closed her eyes and slid the phone into her pocket as she wondered for the millionth time why it had to be so difficult talking to her father. A simple word of praise, an inkling of tenderness, was that so much to ask. She no longer feared her father as she use to as a child. At least, when she was a little girl, she believed his strength protected her. As an adult, she had lost that sensation. And right now, that strong support would have helped, if only she could ask.

The hotel phone jangled, startling her

"Ms. Cabot, the shuttle has left for the airport." *My prayers are answered.*

Zeke began to pace, she was both excited and nervous. She straightened her collar and felt the hot skin on her neck. From the moment she left Albuquerque nearly a week before, Zeke had dreamt about seeing Anne again.

Their short but intense relationship awakened some

deep-seated feelings of passion, desire, and longing. Zeke smiled, wiped her damp hands on her jeans, and welcomed the glowing warmth that began to spread from her center.

It was almost nine when Zeke heard a soft tap at the door. She lunged to get the door open before the third tap. Anne Reynolds looked breathtaking.

They both stared for a moment and then Zeke stepped aside while the bellhop placed a small carry on just inside the door.

Anne tipped him then stepped inside and closed the door turning to Zeke. "Hi, you."

"Annie, I'm so glad you're here." Every muscle in Zeke's body vibrated with excitement.

"Me too. I don't quite know what to say. Isn't that silly?"

"I have a thousand things to tell you and ask you—but mostly I want to wrap you in my arms and pull you inside me where we don't have to talk."

Anne laughed nervously and unzipped her jacket. "I know I'm torn between asking you every single question I've had for seven days, thirteen hours and thirty-three minutes—or tearing off every stitch of your clothing to get at your incredible body and cover it with kisses."

"Hmm, your second plan sounds so much better." She reached for Anne's jacket, tossed it on the chair, and slipped her shaking arms around Anne's waist. "I have missed you so much. God, it feels good to hold you." She inhaled Anne's familiar scent and closed her eyes. They held on tight, neither wishing to break the connection. Zeke drew strength from the safety of this wonderful woman's embrace, unlike any she'd ever known. Her arms tightened.

"Zeke, you feel so good, are you back to stay?"

Anne moved her hands to Zeke's face and caressed it.

"Yes. I have to kiss you." Zeke moved slowly until their lips brushed. The fluttering in her chest grew and desire surged through her.

"I feel like I've waited a lifetime for this very moment," Anne whispered.

Their lips met with passion and pleasure—without restraint or regret, renewing the tastes and textures they had explored so intimately. They kissed long and with delicacy and a teasing longing like a parched throat sensing cool water. The intensity increased quickly and their pulses raced to a point of longing and desire that was becoming urgent, but they slowed themselves to savor each moment of renewal. This reunion was more than a homecoming. The interruption of their intense new relationship had caused each pain. The separation made it worse.

"Wait—let's stop," Anne said, breathing heavily. "I want you so badly right now, but please, let's slow down."

Zeke looked at her. "Is everything all right?" The cold spot began to reform in the center of her chest.

Anne moved her fingertips to Zeke's lips and smiled. "Oh, everything is wonderful." She lightly stroked Zeke's face then cupped her cheek. "I've dreamed of this moment and as hard as it is, I don't want to rush. Please talk to me, tell me how you are, and what happened in Chicago." She pulled Zeke to the bed.

The surge of adrenaline and impending panic subsided. For a millisecond, Zeke had actually believed Anne would leave her. She watched as Anne kicked off her shoes, fluffed the pillows, and nestled herself in while patting the bed beside her. The warmth returned to her chest. "Would you like something to drink?"

"Is there any wine in that little fridge?"

Zeke brought them both a glass of wine and sat back against the headboard. "You'd really rather talk?"

Anne's warm laugh softened the mood. "Yes, I really do. I want to understand what happened in Chicago and I want to know how you are. Then, I'm going to make you so sorry you ever asked that question."

Her sparkling eyes and playful smile told Zeke she had nothing to fear.

"The trip was good. As soon as I arrived in Chicago, I began to miss you insanely. It didn't take long before I was up to my ass in paperwork, financial reports, and bureau analyses. Agent Hartbrooke put together a small task force to dig up background information. It was tedious and frustrating, mostly because I thought I was through with the case. But he was right and they needed my help deciphering the data." She ran her fingers down Anne's arm and hand.

"I was the only one available because the detective on our case was killed in a hit and run a couple of weeks ago." Zeke stopped and took a swallow of wine. That was about as much detail as she wanted to give in spite of her misgivings about the so-called accident. Anne didn't need to know the particulars about the two brothers involved.

"Did you do anything fun while you were there?" Anne asked.

"I spent time with my friend T.J. Montgomery and her partner Cheryl. Whenever I need a reality check, T.J. is the one to give it to me." Zeke smiled at the memory. "She busted my chops for not bringing you along."

Anne's lips curved and her eyebrows quirked up with a 'and what did you say?' kind of expression.

"I know. I just, this just wasn't the time. T.J. also pushed me hard to see a psychiatrist. It was the same woman I saw before I left Chicago."

Anne looped her arm through Zeke's arm and took her hand. "How did that go?"

The processors in Zeke's head kicked into high gear. How much did she want to share at this point? How much was relevant? It seemed a little early in a relationship to tell your lover that you might have a problem with PTSD. Zeke leaned over and pressed a kiss to Anne's temple.

"She thinks that anxiety is affecting my sleep and wants me to take a prescription. She also gave me the name of a doctor in Albuquerque to see for follow up."

Anne just looked at her with an odd expression. Her sky blue eyes seemed to penetrate Zeke's imagined barrier. "Was that all she said?"

"Pretty much, she gave me some complicated psychobabble about brain chemistry and stuff." Zeke reached for Anne's chin and tipped it forward for a gentle kiss. "Now, you tell me what you did while I was gone." She wanted to change the subject because telling a nurse inexact clinical details was like playing with fire.

Anne kissed Zeke back then hopped off the bed. She pulled two more small bottles from the refrigerator and returned to the bed. "As near as I can recall, I sat on the couch in the family room and stared at the beautiful bouquet you sent me and cried gigantic crocodile tears every day. I looked pathetic," she said with her eyes twinkling.

Zeke nodded her head. "I'm sure. Now tell me the truth."

Anne shook her head and adopted a very serious expression. "All right, I wasn't going to tell you, but as hard as I tried, I couldn't stand it. So, two days after you left, I went down to Albuquerque." She took a deep breath and then a swallow of wine. "I found an adult bookstore and I bought sex toys." Anne burst out laughing.

Zeke set her wineglass on the bedside table and pulled Anne's body close to her. "I've missed you so much." She trailed her fingers through the blond lock that had escaped the barrette and stroked the side of Anne's face. It was exactly as she visualized it every night during her stay in Chicago. Anne's pale skin with a hint of color from the sun, soft rounded cheeks, and full lips were as she remembered and there was the slightest crinkle at the corner of her twinkling blue eyes.

"Can I tell you something, Zeke?" Her voice caught. "I was a little afraid you weren't coming back."

Zeke nodded. "I know. I was afraid, too. I understand what I have to do now and I hope you'll be patient with me. I have to find my way back and it's going to take some work." She cleared her throat, took a breath, and braced herself to explain the reason for the trip to Arizona. "Today, I talked to former Agent Sandra Spinelli. In fact, we spent most of the day talking. My boss suggested I talk to her because she had an experience similar to the one we had—only much worse. We compared stories and she told me how hard it was for her to recover from her injuries."

Zeke shifted her position until Anne's head, tucked under her chin, rested on her shoulder. "Some kids in an LA gang assaulted and beat her. It was years ago, but it really messed up her life." Zeke closed her eyes and leaned her head back. "God, it was awful to hear her describe it. She's okay today, but it made me realize how lucky I was." She watched her fingers stroke the soft silk fabric of Anne's blouse at her shoulder. Beneath the thin fabric, she could feel the muscle and the warm skin. She took a deep breath, inhaling the familiar scent of Anne's warm skin, her hair, and the lingering scent of her perfume. Zeke leaned over and pressed a kiss to the top of her head.

"Annie, what freaked me out was the thought of being unable to protect myself and more importantly, protect you. It scared the hell out of me thinking that could happen again and that I was worthless. I understand that now and why I thought I had to run away."

Anne was shaking her head. "How could you possibly have known that would happen? There was nothing you could do—the man had a gun. Zeke, I never doubted you."

"I'm so glad to hear you say that because you're so important to me."

Anne rolled up on her side, and snuggled close. "I want this to work, Zeke Cabot, no matter how hard we have to try.

"I promise I will do whatever it takes." Zeke cupped Anne's head and drew her mouth close. The earlier tenderness changed to intense desire. Zeke's appetite had been wetted and her kiss declared her hunger. She sat up on one knee, grabbed the back of her shirt collar, and yanked it over her head.

Anne's eyes were wide, her pupils dilated.

Zeke could hear her own coarse breathing over the shrieking of an emergency vehicle in the distance.

Above that, Anne's hoarse voice. "Make love to me. Now."

Chapter Five

Anne was awake before the sun peeked through the crack in the room-darkening drapes. She lay on her side watching her lover sleep. Zeke was on her back, the sheet barely covered her chest. One leg was crooked and stuck out from the covers. It was all Anne could do to keep from touching her. The soft pale brown skin beckoned her fingers, but she resisted.

Zeke had been restless much of the night. For the past hour, she had lain still with an angelic look on her face. Anne worried about the sleepless nights. She knew that there were things that Zeke was not ready to tell her, and she would just have to be patient. In time, when Zeke felt safe enough, she would share whatever it was that haunted her. All she could do now was be there to support her.

She rested her cheek on her palm and felt a small smile. However withdrawn Zeke might be with the details of her life, when she made love she was a different person. Anne could still feel the heat in her belly. Satisfied didn't begin to explain the ecstasy she felt. Her lover was gentle and strong, but she was also a patient and demanding. Anne shivered thinking about the number of times Zeke maneuvered her to the edge of sanity until she let go of everything and surrendered.

†

When Anne stepped out of the shower, she received a warm towel, a warm embrace, and a soft kiss.

"I'm going down and work out for about half an hour before breakfast and I'll meet you in the dining room," Zeke said. "Although...I'm enjoying the kissing enough to think about skipping the gym for a different kind of workout."

Anne laughed and responded to the soft, warm lips. "If I'd known you wanted to work out, I'd have gone with you."

"I'll wait if you want—"

"No, go ahead you probably need to burn off some energy, if you have any left," she said and winked. "I'll meet you in the coffee shop."

Anne took her time picking out something to wear. She brought two new outfits, hoping Zeke would like them. When she found the gym on the first floor, Zeke was working on the weight equipment. Unable to contain her smile, Anne stood at the door and watched.

Zeke increased the amount of weight on her machine and continued pulling down the curved bar connected to the heavy steel bars—flexing and extending. After changing her hand position, she repeated the reps.

Anne smiled. In her normal street clothes, Zeke appeared to be an attractive woman who was tall and lean. In short-shorts and a tight tank top—lifting weights, it was very clear that the leanness was indeed muscle. Zeke's sculptured torso moved fluidly with each pull of the bar. The clearly defined muscles in her back and shoulders glistened with perspiration. Anne watched with amazement and deep appreciation for the strong and tender woman who made her spirit soar. It was good to see her working her body. Maybe she really had turned a corner in her healing.

She took a step back into the hallway and headed

to the restaurant. The sudden return trip to Chicago had worried Anne because, from her clinical perspective, Zeke had grown depressed and withdrawn. They needed to talk more and there would be time. But, in the interim, their rekindled chemistry and the desire intoxicated her. These feelings were still relatively new to her and extremely heady. In all her years with Andrew, she had never experienced this level of sexual freedom and joy.

During Zeke's absence, Anne scoured her past memories for instances when she might have had an attraction to another woman. It was possible. Some of the friendships in her early adolescence had been intense. Were they sexual? She wasn't sure. There was no denying the attraction now, none whatsoever.

At precisely nine a.m., Zeke arrived to meet Anne at the coffee shop. She had showered, dressed, and was looking very self satisfied and quite stunning. The waves in her dark brown hair still damp and shiny hung just above the collar of her warm-up jacket.

"Good morning." She slid into the booth across from Anne and pulled the napkin into her lap. "Have you ordered?"

"Just coffee, I wanted to wait for you," Anne grinned.

Zeke looked down at her clothing and back to Anne. "Did I forget to button something?"

"No, I'm just really glad to see you."

"And I am really glad to see you," Zeke said. A warm smile revealed her gleaming white teeth framed by very soft and expressive lips and the irresistible dimple. Without any makeup, Zeke's strong mocha-brown face glowed, the color accented by her hypnotic amber flecked brown eyes.

As if on cue, a short waitress, who looked exactly

like Rhea Perlman, arrived and took their order then returned with more coffee.

"So the meeting yesterday—did you learn anything else or would you rather not talk about it?"

Zeke looked up.

"No, that's okay. The after-effects of Sandra's ordeal were rotten. Her husband divorced her, her partner asked for a transfer, and she spent months in rehab. It was grueling, but she did it. I really admire what she did."

"Sounds like you've made a new friend." Anne knew her tone sounded sarcastic and she tried to compensate. "I'm happy you had a chance to share this with someone who can actually understand." Anne wondered why Zeke wanted to talk to a stranger instead of confiding in her. After all, she was a trained professional, too. She bit her lower lip and said nothing further.

"I'm really grateful for the advice and, of course, her willingness to talk about a really painful chapter in her life," Zeke paused. "Sandra provided some really critical insights, from an agent's point of view, that even Dr. Nilsson couldn't have known." She stirred cream into her coffee and continued. "For all of the support I've gotten from well-intentioned friends, no one has really understood—except Sandra. And knowing she survived and has pretty much moved past it without permanent scarring has helped a great deal." Zeke, seemingly embarrassed, stopped. "Wow, that was a bit of a ramble, sorry."

"Don't be. I wanted to know how you are," Anne forced a smile.

"Great. She wants to meet you and I told her we could have dinner with her." Zeke said. Just then, their food arrived and she plunged into a stack of pancakes enthusiastically.

Anne looked on amazed at Zeke's gusto and started picking at her omelet. This was a new person—reenergized and lively. It was very attractive. The niggling question remained, who had ignited this live wire? Zeke looked different, but Anne's inner voice warned her to be careful of the new stranger. Something felt off and she couldn't put a finger on it.

They ate in silence for a few minutes until Zeke laid her knife and fork on the clean plate and wiped her mouth, then sighed.

"Feel like taking a walk?" Anne asked.

†

After grabbing their jackets for the cool autumn day, they set out to explore the local area. Once away from the hotel, Zeke asked, "We've talked about me—how have you been?"

"Fine, I worked a few days in the south valley for another nurse who is on vacation. We closed our case on the patient from the Jemez Pueblo. I didn't press charges against the two boys because no one was hurt but there were a couple of serious thefts at the same time and so there was a court case. Mrs. Padilla's grandsons got probation and community service because of their ages but the older boys got jail time. I don't expect I'll be welcomed back anytime soon."

"That was unfortunate, but those kids got off easy."

Anne began to relax as they wandered through a small quaint shopping mall, browsing the unusual shops and picking up an occasional item. Anne agreed to dinner with Sandra for that evening, although she would have preferred to keep Zeke to herself.

†

While Zeke phoned Sandra to confirm dinner later, Anne went down to confer with the concierge. He provided several options including car rentals, train and bus connections, as well as helicopter and plane tours. She explained that they had only one day.

The concierge pulled a couple of specific brochures. "The Eco Star Helicopter is reportedly a very enjoyable trip and has excellent views of the Canyon—but it is pricey, $190 per person for a fifty minute flight and then there is transportation to and from the park. Another very popular option is the Grand Canyon Railroad Excursion. We have had very good feedback on this. They will pick you up here and drive you to Williams where you will board an antique train for an interesting ride to the park then have lunch followed by a bus tour of the South Rim-some free time and a return trip. It's a long day but quite memorable."

Anne returned to the room to find Zeke still talking with Sandra. As hard as she tried, she found herself once again fighting off feelings of anxiety and jealousy. She smiled and took the brochures to the table and sat down.

"Great. We'll meet you at six-thirty p.m....no, don't think about it. We'll cab over. Bye." Zeke hung up and walked over to the table. She bent down and kissed Anne's neck and ear while she moved her hand along the top of her shoulders and down her arms. "What did you find out?"

Anne felt her silly resistance to Zeke's new friend start to melt as Zeke continued to rub her neck and shoulders. She spread out the brochures and repeated what the concierge had told her.

Zeke looked the brochures over. "Well, given our

limited time, I think one of the inclusive tours would be best. It will take a couple of hours to get up there."

Anne tipped her head forward and Zeke continued to rub before raking her hair gently with her fingers.

"That helicopter trip looks incredible," Zeke said.

"The down side is that it's only fifty minutes and costs almost $200 per person. I think that's too much money. Plus, there would be transportation to and from the park."

"Annie, this was my great scheme and I'll pay for it. You had to pay for the plane fare out here. I can afford it and I want to." Zeke turned Anne's face and kissed her mouth firmly and deeply.

Anne savored the faint taste of maple syrup and felt the familiar tug in her belly that signaled desire and she moaned softly.

Zeke broke away and began to read the brochures.

After reviewing a few more, they decided on the Railroad excursion. Anne walked over to the bedside phone, called down to the concierge desk, and made the reservation while Zeke stretched out on the bed next to her. As she hung up, Zeke patted the bed next to her and without hesitation; Anne curled up beside her, welcoming the embrace and the slow, deep kisses.

Nestled close to Zeke, Anne could hear the steady heartbeat that she had missed so much. The soft fabric of Zeke's shirt warmed her cheek.

"Annie are you okay, you seem a little sad or something?"

"Well, you seem different somehow and I'm not sure what that means."

"What exactly is different? I'm here and I'm thrilled to see you. I'm not magically cured, but I finally feel like there's a light at the end of the tunnel." Zeke sounded puzzled.

"You just seemed so excited about spending the day with Sandra and the fact that you wanted to see her before you saw me…I guess I felt like an afterthought."

Zeke pulled back a little and smiled. "You're jealous!" She laughed.

Anne sat up abruptly. "Maybe I am. I hadn't thought of it that way." Her voice sounded tight and angry to her.

Zeke reached for her hand, but Anne just sat up abruptly on the side of the bed.

"Okay. Let's talk." Zeke shook her head. "I think I explained why I came here first. I wanted to clear up more of the 'baggage' as I promised, before I saw you. You specifically told me not to come back until I was whole. You did not want 'an empty shell' as you put it." Zeke moved to her side. "I wanted to come back to your bed as whole and healed as I could possibly be. The healing isn't finished and I'm sorry. But I couldn't wait any longer to be with you."

Anne didn't know what to say. Her heart thudded loudly and her stomach churned.

"Are you even listening to me?"

"You're right." Anne couldn't sit still and jumped up. Pacing helped. "I did say those things and I wanted to give you time to heal…but…it was so damn hard." The room was suddenly small and airless. Anne stood behind one of the chairs to have something to hold. "I had no idea how badly I had fallen for you until you were gone. All I could do in your absence was create terrible images of you with other women and yes, be jealous." Anne turned to face the window. Her voice softened. "I didn't plan on falling in love with you or anyone."

Zeke remained seated on the bed, dumbstruck. Was she really that upset about Sandra? What happened to the strong, capable independent woman who had saved her life and prevented her from slipping off the edge during the darkest hours? Fear inched up her spine. There were twinkly lights—*Anne's voice is growing fainter like an echo. Walls are moving in—closing in then retreating. Dizzy. What's happening?*

When Anne got no response, she turned to see Zeke staring at her with a very strange expression on her face—a mix of confusion, anger, disbelief, and fear. She could only look briefly before she gathered her wits and let go of her emotional rant to see that something was wrong.

"Zeke...are you all right?"

No answer.

"Zeke please say something. I'm worried—"

Anne crossed quickly to the bed and knelt in front of her. Zeke's eyes seemed focused on a distant point outside the window, but it didn't look as if she was seeing anything. Anne squeezed her hands, no reaction. She tried snapping her fingers and clapping her hands, no response. Breathing and pulses were slow and regular, her color fair and suddenly she gasped and collapsed onto her right side. Anne lifted her legs onto the bed and sat beside her, held her hand and watched as her eyes fluttered and began to focus. "You're okay," Anne whispered, "it's all right."

Zeke turned her head, looking confused. "What just happened?"

"I'm not sure, but I think you may have had a little seizure".

"What?"

"It's called a petite mal seizure. It only lasts a few moments where you mentally shut down without a real loss of consciousness, kind of like a short circuit. Not harmful."

Anne stood up and started for the bathroom. "Just rest, I'll get some water."

Anne returned to find Zeke asleep. She set the water on the table, picked up Zeke's hand, and waited. When Zeke awakened, it was getting dark. "You are certainly an unpredictable little thing." Anne smiled and kissed her cheek softly.

"Am I okay or is this a new condition that'll screw up my life?"

"I'm sure you're fine. But we can get it checked out when we get back to New Mexico. Trauma or stress can sometimes cause those little black-out episodes. Do you remember it ever happening before, any unexplained loss of time? People acting like you aren't paying attention?"

"No, I don't think so, no one ever mentioned it. Is it permanent?"

Anne rolled onto her side and put her arm around Zeke's waist, "It may never happen again in your life." She paused. "Zeke, I'm sorry for behaving so childishly. I was wrong, you made no promises to me, and I have no right to be so possessive. I'd like to meet your friend. Let's go have a nice dinner and enjoy our weekend."

Zeke reached up and stroked Anne's face, looked into her eyes, and stroked her lower lip with her thumb. With no words, she kissed the lips she was touching.

Anne kept one eye on Zeke as they each dressed for dinner. The unexpected seizure alarmed her more than she let on and she wanted to make sure she didn't miss any other symptoms. It may have just come after an intense day discussing their trauma. She really didn't understand what all happened in Chicago either. Maybe it was stressful and maybe Zeke wasn't taking good care of herself. It would bear watching.

†

In the cab on the way to the restaurant, Anne sat close to Zeke with her right hand on Zeke's leg while the driver extolled the virtues of 'Blix'—the restaurant they had chosen. Anne made up her mind to behave cordially toward Zeke's friend.

Sandra Spinelli was waiting in the lobby and Anne smiled with relief when she saw the non- threatening retired special agent. "It's nice to meet you. Zeke spoke so highly of you." Anne extended her hand.

"It's nice to meet you too. Zeke, hello again."

The maitre d' escorted them to a table and the waiter appeared to hold the chairs for each. After hearing the specials, they ordered a bottle of pinot noir, recommended by the sommelier.

"What kind of nursing do you practice?" Sandra turned the conversation to Anne.

Anne appreciated the gesture, knowing the two women sitting with her shared some personal revelations twenty-four hours earlier. "I work part time as a home health nurse for one of our local agencies. I cover the northern part of our territory including Rio Rancho and Bernalillo." Anne put her glass down and glanced quickly at Zeke who was smiling broadly.

"I have always admired nurses for the work they do and their dedication. A noble profession that those of us who work in law enforcement hold in very high esteem." Sandra lifted her glass toward Anne.

Zeke responded in kind, "I will certainly second that," and squeezed Anne's hand.

"Do you ever worry when you're out driving around? I mean, don't you have to go into some rather questionable neighborhoods?" asked Sandra.

"Yes and no. That seems to be a common question and I'd have to say, no matter where I go, there is an overall acceptance of nurses. It seems that people like knowing that we're around if a family member or neighbor needs medical assistance. Although," she glanced at Zeke, "there was a nasty incident a few weeks ago that involved the grandkids of a patient. As it happened, there was a wonderful FBI agent who rescued me." Anne winked at Zeke.

The leisurely dinner was excellent and accompanied by lighter topics about the locale and the pending trip to the Grand Canyon. Sandra agreed that they had made a wise choice with the Railroad excursion.

The inevitable agency talk, which Anne expected, took up a fair amount of the conversations. Both Sandra and Zeke agreed they'd like to stay in touch. Sandra insisted on picking up the check and Zeke finally demurred. Since Sandra's car was close, she offered to drive them back even though Zeke argued with her. In the end, Sandra won out and dropped them off at the hotel. Zeke was clearly flexing a little muscle and so was Sandra. Anne simply watched with amusement but wondered if this was typical behavior among agents.

†

When they finally reached their room, it was late. The events of the past twenty-four hours ran together and crashed like surf breaking on the rocks. She watched carefully as Zeke went about her nighttime regimen methodically. There must be some Zen-like peace in her deliberate attention to detail. It seldom varied. When she climbed into their bed, Anne snuggled against the beautiful woman lying next to her.

Her newfound passion for this alluring woman overrode her usual vigilance and sensibilities. She needed to learn more. The Zeke Cabot who returned from Chicago seemed somehow different. After watching her interact with another agent left her with more questions than answers.

Chapter Six

The Grand Canyon shuttle arrived on time and whisked Zeke and Anne off for their excursion along with three others from a nearby hotel—an older couple with a younger woman who was introduced as their daughter. There was the usual conversation regarding jobs and hometowns. The Klein's were visiting from New York looking to find a warmer place to live. They gushed at the FBI Agent and the Home Health Nurse '—such wonderful jobs and so important.' As the van continued along the busy interstate, conversation diminished as passengers hypnotically watched the vast desert spread out endlessly around them. Zeke slipped Anne's hand into her own and smiled.

"Are you amused by something?" Anne asked somewhat embarrassed

"Not exactly." Zeke turned to face her. "Just happy."

When they reached the railroad station, there was a noticeable increase in activity. Dozens of people milled around on the platform by an antique steam engine. The coal-fired engine was spewing black smoke in large puffs. The train was a beautiful reminder of a more elegant time and an especially memorable time in the old west.

"This is incredible." Zeke's eyes looked just like the eyes of the children standing nearby.

There were several families but most of the tourists waiting were older and not in as much of a hurry as the younger ones. Anne held Zeke's elbow to let everyone pass them. She wanted time to savor this experience not knowing what lay before them.

The van driver handed them tickets and when the boarding began, the mob moved forward as a unit.

Zeke took Anne's arm and guided her toward the rear. They entered the last car and sat in the last seat. When all were aboard, the last car was only partially full.

The voice of the conductor/guide began with a welcome, instructions, and warnings about dangers. He indicated the locations of bathrooms and the approximate travel time. He also mentioned the availability of blankets as the train had no heat and October weather changed quickly.

The whistle blew and the chugging sounds of the shiny black and gold engine began as the old train pulled out.

"Here we go," said Zeke with her brown eyes twinkling.

"Yes, you had a really good idea, I'm glad I'm here." Anne blinked and her eyes began to tear.

The windows afforded an excellent view as they headed toward the Grand Canyon. The guide, who continued his dialogue, almost nonstop, dutifully described each different climate zones and landmarks.

Passengers snapped photos and videos. It became quieter as the desert faded and the train began its ascent, the mountains were visible on both sides of the train.

Zeke pulled a blanket from the overhead brass luggage rack and covered them both. Anne smiled in appreciation as Zeke surreptitiously took her hand and began a slow and intentional touching, rubbing, and interlocking of their fingers that became more and more sensual. Neither spoke. Anne closed her eyes and relished the soft sensuous feeling of Zeke's strong fingers.

The guide droned over the speakers and the tourists looked out the windows snapping pictures. Zeke continued her mission of stealth by pulling Anne's hand onto her covered lap and explored every cubic centimeter of her lover's hand resting on her thigh. They missed some of the spectacular scenery, lost as they were in the wonder of each other.

Anne felt the butterflies flittering wildly as powerful waves of warmth enveloped her belly. Twice she glanced around wishing for more privacy to intensify the rapidly escalating blaze between them. Perspiration dampened her forehead and the area between her breasts. Anne closed her eyes and rolled her head to one side as an intense wave of heat enveloped her whole body. She desperately wanted every stitch of clothing gone and wanted Zeke's hot hands on her naked flesh.

When she was composed and able to speak, Anne sat up, removed the stifling blanket, and looked crossly at Zeke. "You are a very bad person!"

Zeke took her hand and kissed it softly. "I know."

†

When the elegant steam engine pulled into the station at the Grand Canyon National Park, it created a flurry of excitement with passengers scurrying in several directions trying to find bathrooms, gift shops or whatever, before they had to meet for a quick lunch then off to the bus for the canyon viewing.

Zeke and Anne just strolled, enjoying the time together without expectation. It was a sunny and cool October day in the desert. Around them trees were turning gold and a few leaves blew across the parking lot and sidewalks.

Outside the visitor center, they found a bench and Anne said, "Wait here, I'll be right back."

Zeke watched her walk quickly toward the gift shop with a strong purposeful gait and a very nice ass, well toned from horseback riding. During her time in Chicago, she could only fantasize about the beautiful body walking away from her. The reality was so much better than her fantasies. She couldn't help but smile thinking about the way her own body reacted and then a dark sadness washed over her.

It had only been two weeks since the assault and the memory flooded back for just one horrible moment. *Damn those bastards.* Regularly occurring nightmares—already robbing her of sleep—began to sneak in during the day. Vigilance around large men added another wrinkle. Accidental touches by any stranger caused an exaggerated reaction.

Zeke understood that only time would help. Sandra warned her about the possibility of flashbacks, but Zeke hated the panic episodes and fear.

She didn't want Anne to worry so she kept it to herself. But eventually, Anne would notice something and Zeke would need to be honest. It was hard since their relationship was so new. She hoped that her weird behavior wouldn't scare Anne off. *Let it go.* With a deep breath, she began to relax.

When she heard loud voices behind her, Zeke looked over her shoulder and saw a young man and woman off the path near some trees. The man was yelling and the woman kept pulling away. He was holding her by the shoulders and shaking her and then struck her, rocking her head back. The woman started to run and he quickly grabbed her by the hair and threw her down to the ground.

Zeke responded instantly by leaping off the bench and dashing toward the couple. Before she knew it, she stood between the two. "Step back and leave her alone," she ordered. When the male took a step back, she reached down to help the woman to her feet.

"Mind your own fucking business." The bully upped the ante and took a step forward.

Zeke shook with fury. The man was short—5'5" or 5'6"—and was clearly angry. Zeke's fingers were clenched and she desperately wanted to beat him senseless, but pulled back just in time. She removed her badge and ID from her pocket and swung it into the man's face. "I am a Federal Agent, and you have just committed a felony assault." Her right hand was reaching for the handle of her automatic. "Don't make me hurt you." A crowd started to gather.

†

Anne came out of the gift shop just as Zeke flew off the bench toward the couple and rushed over at the same time as a Security Guard appeared.

The young woman shook with fear so Anne moved over to her and gently ushered her away from the conflict.

The Security Guard radioed for assistance and Zeke explained what had occurred.

After taking Zeke's report and contact information, Security escorted both the man and woman away. Zeke and Anne moved away from the scene as word of the incident spread through the crowd.

"Are you all right?" asked Anne once they were out of earshot.

"Yes." Zeke's arms hugged her body. "I don't

know what happened. I heard the yelling and saw him hit her and I lost it for a second. As soon as I pulled my ID, sanity returned. It was weird."

"I can't leave you alone for a minute before you get yourself in hot water." Anne smiled. On the inside, she was anything but smiling.

†

After lunch, they boarded the sightseeing bus and drove along the South rim of the canyon stopping at several lookouts for pictures.

Zeke sat mesmerized by the beauty. The grandeur of the canyon was almost impossible to describe in words. It was immense in size and with an almost sacred and pervasive feeling. Most of the visitors were silent or barely whispering, so awed were they by the overwhelming size and beauty. The colors of the ancient etched canyon changed with the desert light and clouds. It was truly breathtaking and all the more so when shared with someone else. Everyone took dozens of photos—none of which would capture the remarkable immensity of the place.

†

They boarded the train back to Williams, Arizona, in the late afternoon. Zeke noticed the ride back was more subdued as the tourists had run out of steam and so had the guide.

Suddenly, Anne was rummaging through her bag. "In all the excitement I completely forgot that I got you a souvenir—" She produced a tissue wrapped item.

Zeke took it and smiled, surprised at the thoughtful gesture. It was a black baseball cap embroidered with a

69

picture of the Grand Canyon. Zeke laughed and put it on. "I love it! And I'll never take it off." She leaned over to give Anne a hug.

"There's something else for you." Anne produced a smaller box.

Zeke stopped grinning when she noticed the serious tone in Anne's voice. She carefully took the small box, and then opened it. There was a sterling silver key chain holding a single key. Her mind erupted with a thousand thoughts and her heart responded with a flood of emotions. Zeke felt her stomach drop as she found herself slammed into reality. She was voluntarily making a huge leap into a brand new responsibility. "Are you sure you want to do this?"

"More than anything." Anne wrapped her arms around Zeke's neck.

For what seemed like the first time, Zeke experienced someone loving her, caring for her, and scaring her all at the same time. She knew she couldn't do it alone. It would be hard for both of them and she fervently hoped Anne would not leave her. She laced fingers through Anne's and squeezed her hand.

†

After a brief stop in Williams for a sandwich and the long ride back to Flagstaff, Zeke and Anne finally collapsed in bed exhausted but happy. Zeke knew that the next day was the trip to Albuquerque and back to 'real life'.

Chapter Seven

Zeke called to confirm the flight reservations for Albuquerque and finished dressing. She hung up and walked to the bathroom door where Anne stood applying makeup. "I'm hungry. Can we go eat first and pack later?"

Anne looked up at the reflection in the mirror and smiled. "Of course we can. I'm just trying to look presentable so I don't embarrass you."

Zeke kissed her neck. "You never embarrass me."

†

The waitress approached them with the coffee pot. "Yes, I'd like a little more," said Anne. "Thank you."

When Zeke looked up, her jaw dropped as a very tall woman dressed as Carmen Miranda, including the fruit basket on her head leaned over to pour refills.

She smiled and moved her cup to the edge of the table. "Thanks." Her gaze followed the strange vision as the waitress sashayed away. "What was that?"

Anne put her cup down and shook her head. "Well, it's Halloween and maybe that's a big deal out here."

"Damn. It scared the hell out me," Zeke said. She added cream to her coffee and stirred it slowly.

"Who's Sheila" Anne asked.

Huh? Crap. Zeke could feel her pulse accelerate. Uncertain about how to answer this question, she stalled by sipping her coffee. "Beg your pardon?"

Anne precisely spread some orange marmalade on

her toast. "You must have had a bad dream last night because you called out her name, quite loudly."

"Really? Sheila, huh. I guess it could have been Shayla." The jack-hammering in her chest increased. Zeke looked around nervously.

Anne laughed lightly. "All right. Who's Shayla? Is this a friend of yours or an ex-lover?" Her expression tightened. "Maybe it's someone you saw in Chicago?"

It required too much energy for Zeke to make up a story. "When I was taken to the hospital after I got hit by the truck in July, Shayla Graham was my doctor. Since I was working undercover, I had no ID with me and had to be admitted as a Jane Doe." Zeke cleared her throat. "One of the staff nurses was involved with our case as a C.I., uh, confidential informant recognized me—fortunately. She notified the FBI field office. Long story short, I had to explain a little bit of my undercover job to the doctor so she could keep it under wraps."

Leaning back in the booth, she continued. "It turned out that Dr. Graham was a senior surgical resident and worked for the very physician we believed to be our primary suspect. He actually 'hired' her to help with the research project with the cadaver heads." Zeke's hands began to tremble and she put them in her lap. "She practiced his surgical technique on them. It was because of her help that we were able to put the pieces together. His cadaver heads came from the murdered homeless victims. She got us enough proof to get an arrest." The excruciating memories flooded back.

"Are you all right?"

Zeke shook her head and took a breath. "They murdered her."

Anne gasped.

All the sounds of the restaurant faded. Zeke closed

her eyes and consciously slowed her breathing. *I will not lose it.*

An eerie silence hung over the emergency room when the FBI agents arrived. They had heard the radio call that another decapitated body turned up.

When Zeke entered through the air-lock doors, she spotted their contact nurse, Kate Ramsey, sitting on the floor in the doorway of trauma room ten sobbing hysterically.

"What's going on?" Zeke asked a surgical resident standing nearby.

Zeke noticed other staff members standing around, some staring wide eyed while others cried quietly. The body on the gurney lay partially covered with one foot exposed.

The resident swiped at his eyes. "It's one of our senior residents, she was just brought in. Why would anyone want to hurt her?" he mumbled.

Detective Shapiro was standing at the desk.

Zeke asked, "Hey, Dan, what have you got?"

"Good to see you, Cabot. Not much, there was no ID because, like the others, the head and hands were missing. That nurse over there," he pointed at Kate Ramsey, "recognized her because of the tattoo on her ankle." He flipped a page in his notebook, "name is— Graham, Shayla Graham. Seems like she was a pretty popular resident."

A wave of nausea threatened and Zeke pulled the napkin into her mouth. Her head was spinning and blinking spots danced behind her eyelids.

Anne slid over to her side. "Take a deep breath. That's good."

Zeke could feel Anne's warm hand rubbing her

back and she took the offered water glass with both hands. She choked at the first sip and tried again. The muscles in her throat began to cooperate and the water made its way past her tightened throat. The searing ache in her chest was almost unbearable.

Anne looked at the check on the table, peeled off several bills, and left them. "Let's go."

Zeke slid out of the booth and tried to stand on rubbery legs. It was hard to focus but she could feel Anne's strong fingers holding her elbow and pushing her toward the door. She saw the elevator door close and the numbers flash in front of her until they get to the fifth floor. Anne's strong arm was around her waist and she saw the green light flash on the door lock.

"I want you to lie down for a little while, okay?"

Zeke nodded and sat down on the bed.

Anne lifted her legs up onto the bed and removed her shoes. "You're okay, baby, I'm right here and I'm not going to leave."

With her eyes closed, Zeke's breathing began to slow. Anne was holding her and stroking her forehead allowing the knot in her chest to loosen.

†

The courtesy car was waiting for them. The brief nap had helped and while she slept, Anne had packed their belongings. Zeke was feeling better, at least physically. She was able to follow simple instructions to get in and out of the vehicle, carry luggage, and produce identification. The commuter plane departed on time and after a short hop; they arrived in Phoenix for a two-hour layover.

While Zeke's grandmother had staunchly believed there were angels among us, Zeke never gave it much credence, until now. She looked at the wonderful woman standing in front of her at the airline counter. Mortal or angel, Zeke felt very grateful. She moved a little closer and lightly touched Anne's back feeling the soft cotton shirt and the warm skin beneath—the act soothed the rough edges of Zeke's consciousness.

Anne turned and smiled. "All checked in. Let's find a nice place to hang out for a while."

Their assigned gate area was mostly empty and they chose two seats against the wall.

"Would you mind if I went to get a magazine and some coffee?" Anne asked.

"Of course not, I'm okay. Would you get me some Tums? "

As Anne headed back toward the newsstand, Zeke looked out the window at the Phoenix skyline thinking about Hassan's contact man in Phoenix named Abdul Mubarak. He hired the men that followed her and assaulted them. But she didn't understand the connection to Ahmed Hussein. Or, more importantly, why were they so intent on finding her.

She and Detective Shapiro paid little attention to the vast network that was involved with the Hussein brothers 'import' business, because it was unrelated to the murder case. Now, it looked more and more like the younger brother, Hassan Hussein, was the financial wheeler-dealer and used his brother's prestige and reputation, as a professor of surgery, to open doors worldwide.

The import export business initially looked clean. After reviewing the financials on his last trip, it now showed some very questionable connections. Zeke was glad she would no longer be involved with investigating some of the shady characters they found.

Out of nowhere, she remembered the large

envelope that Special Agent in Charge Hartbrooke discussed. Sometime before his 'accidental' death, Detective Shapiro had assembled all of his notes and sent them to Hartbrooke with a note to forward them to Zeke. *Curious.*

Zeke thought he must have had some unanswered suspicions that would cause him to take that precaution. Perhaps if she had seen them sooner—but there was no point in *what-if-ing.*

Anne returned with coffee and a magazine. "Well you look rather ominous." She handed Zeke the coffee.

"Sorry, I was just thinking about the strange Mr. Mubarak." She pointed to the window. "He's out there somewhere and I was wondering if I should have had a chat with him."

"What good would that do except to let him know who you are? Zeke, you need to let the local authorities do their jobs. You're on vacation, remember," Anne said gently.

"Right. Thanks for the coffee."

"You're welcome." She handed Zeke a napkin and the Tums she'd requested.

"Annie, I'm so glad I found you, or more correctly, you found me. I'm not sure I'd have been able to handle this by myself. I get so damn caught up—anyway, thanks." She was grateful that Anne respected her need to crawl in a hole sometimes in order to process and still provided such comfort. She ran the back of her fingers along Anne's cheek. "You have such a natural skill for nurturing and caring. I'm envious. How come you guys never had kids?"

Anne shrugged and looked away. "I wasn't able to."

Zeke sensed that there were more words left hanging as Anne pull back a little. She waited.

Anne took the plastic lid off her cup and blew on the coffee. "I had an abortion when I was twenty-one." She looked up to the large tinted windows and stretched out her legs. "My junior year in college, I went to one of the fraternity parties. We were all drinking some dreadful concoction they mixed up in a garbage can." She shuddered, and sipped her coffee.

Zeke noticed how tight Anne's voice sounded—almost clinical sounding.

"I don't even remember the guy's name or even what he looked like. We were totally wasted and ended up in somebody's bedroom. The noise downstairs was deafening, I still remember the floor vibrating from the huge speakers in the living room. No one even heard me when—" She stopped speaking as a single tear rolled down her cheek.

Zeke sat speechless, only vaguely aware of the flight announcements in the background or the river of passengers scurrying along the concourse.

Anne's voice became softer. "I never told anyone. I was humiliated. I went to Mexico over spring break." Her eyes closed and her head dropped. "It was a horrible experience. Alone in a foreign country where I didn't speak the language. The whole ordeal was impersonal assembly-line medicine. Cold and clinical.

"They put me up in a hot, filthy hotel room. For three days, I was delirious with fever from the post-op infection after they've punctured the wall of the uterus. Permanently scarred after one fucking drunken night." She rummaged through her purse until she found a tissue and blew her nose. "I never told Andrew how the scarring occurred. I never told anyone, ever, until now."

They both sat in silence.

"My God, Annie. I am so sorry." Zeke slipped her arm around Anne's shoulders.

Anne began to cry softly.

Zeke ached for Anne, thinking about the years that she had carried those dark memories all by herself.

Anne wept and Zeke held her tightly.

†

Zeke used the quiet flight time to Albuquerque to ponder dark unseen wounds and the damage those wounds had created. She thought about Anne, the past twenty-four hours, and what they shared. The details were certainly more intimate than those they had shared in the previous month. She found an irony in the gift of finding each other, but it was not something that either could articulate, at least not yet.

Anne had left her car at the airport, which allowed them to leave quickly and get home. Zeke opened the car window as soon as they got on the road and took a deep breath of the crisp New Mexico air. The cool October night smelled like damp leaves, pine trees, and maybe a little piñon smoke. "It's hard to believe I could miss a place so much after only a few weeks." She reached over and took Anne's hand, "I think it really is a land of enchantment."

"It certainly is much nicer with you here." Anne squeezed back.

Zeke kissed the back of her hand and felt pleasure encircle her heart.

†

As soon as they parked the car in the garage and got the luggage in the house, Anne went directly to check her horses. Zeke turned on lights and took the luggage upstairs. She was unpacking her things in the guest room when Anne came upstairs.

"They're fine and happy I'm home. Jeff did a good job. I called Susan and told her we were home," said Anne.

Zeke turned around and embraced her tightly. "We're home, and you know what? I like the sound of that, Annie." Their lips met, Anne wrapped her arms around Zeke's neck, and sighed, savoring their homecoming kiss.

Anne purred. "Have I told you lately that I love the way you taste?"

Zeke sensed a rising kind of urgency, grasped the back of Anne's head, and forced her mouth open with her lips and tongue. A tightly coiled spring deep inside her chest threatened to burst. The kiss fueled by hunger and anger from long buried feelings and fears. Zeke captured Anne's mouth with one fierce kiss after another then stopped.

Zeke understood, on a much deeper level, the intense passion they both shared, and the need for a physical release. Anne's eyes reflected Zeke's intensity.

"We better eat something first," Anne said breathlessly.

Zeke nodded as she held Anne's face with both hands. "If you insist. You do realize you only make the desire more intense?"

Anne grinned and nodded.

†

Dinner was soup and scrambled eggs. "I'll go to the store tomorrow, promise." Anne laughed as she served up the improvised meal.

"This is great. I really don't want anything more." Zeke pushed around the eggs.

"I noticed you haven't been eating much," Anne commented.

"Yeah, not much of an appetite I guess."

"How was it in Chicago?" Anne probed a little further.

"Fair, I guess. Meals were sort of erratic because of all the running around and—you know the emotional roller coaster."

"What do you mean?"

Zeke focused on stirring her soup. "It was hard to go back and revisit the undercover assignment. Just looking at the pictures and reading the reports again, dredged up a lot of bad feelings."

"It sounds like a lot more went on than you've told me."

"I guess it did, but I really can't discuss the details too much."

Anne stood up abruptly and walked over to the sink. She rinsed off her dishes and stuck them in the dishwasher the same way she might stack cordwood, and then turned to face the table. "Zeke, I know you needed to go back because of work. And I believed you when you told me that you needed the time to get your head together." She returned and stood leaning over the table, looking at Zeke.

The trembling started low in Zeke's belly. It was hard to form words and even harder to form coherent thoughts. Sensations of prickly panic coursed through her veins. "Annie, I tried really hard to find some kind of solution, some answer that would allow me to come back to you with answers." She pushed the dishes away from her and looked up into the pale blue eyes filled with concern. "I couldn't do it. At least I couldn't do it there. The whole time I was gone, all I could think about was being back here with you." She clasped her hands together tightly on the table. "The short amount of time you and I shared were some of the happiest I can remember. More importantly, some of the safest."

Anne's lips formed a weak smile. "I'm a little surprised that you would say safe considering the injuries you sustained with me."

Zeke shook her head, remembering the accident on the trail with a rattlesnake. "You have a point. I was thinking more about how I feel inside. Even though I thoroughly enjoyed spending time with T.J. and Cheryl, all I could think about was you and how badly I wanted to be back here." Zeke reached across the table. "I couldn't bear to be away from you, but I promised not to come back until I was healed and whole. Annie, forgive me for not being up front earlier, I didn't have a quick cure. I couldn't do it there or in that short amount of time. I needed to be here with you." Zeke's hands trembled.

Anne's eyes glistened with tears as she clasped both of Zeke's hands. "Oh, baby, I wanted you back here. I never wanted you to leave. When you did, I thought maybe you were having second thoughts. I never realized how hard this was for you. Whatever you need I'll help you and I won't leave you."

"Thank you." Some of the heaviness lifted and Zeke took a breath. The trembling subsided and her body sagged with fatigue. "I'm really tired. Can we go to bed?

†

Anne walked around her house slowly locking doors, turning out lights and then started upstairs.

It had taken years for Anne to get over her husband's arrogance, selfishness, and betrayal. The surprising attraction to this wonderful woman had the potential of unknown dangers or wonderful surprises. Anne had a choice, she could play it safe and avoid the possibility of getting hurt, or she could play full out— dive in headfirst and feel everything, every exquisite moment.

Anne saw that Zeke left her luggage in the guest room as she suggested.

As they each got ready for bed, Anne's mind raced with feelings she repressed. *Fear, love, abandonment, passion, need, anger, tenderness, trust, sharing, lust, forgiveness—* Just seeing Zeke so fragile and so vulnerable after the seizure in Arizona, triggered her protectiveness just as it had when she found Zeke injured on the hiking trail. The seemingly unflappable federal agent—make that, stunningly attractive federal agent—presented as a sophisticated, commanding individual. What lay beneath was far more complex.

Her skin flushed warm as desire and confusion competed for her attention. Anne stripped off her clothes and slipped on her silk robe. As she stood in front of the vanity brushing her hair, she stared at her reflection. Instead of clarity, she noticed the flush in her cheeks. Her skin tingled remembering the embraces and the intimate touches that inflamed her. That was what she really wanted.

Zeke was standing in her worn, torn FBI tee shirt unpacking when Anne came in and touched her hand, turned her around, and kissed her cheeks, neck and throat.

Zeke returned the kisses with urgency.

Anne's need grew as she put her hands on Zeke's waist then moved them to her firm and responsive breasts.

"Come with me you gorgeous hunk of woman."

With Zeke in tow, Anne moved them both to the master bedroom and closed the door with some finality.

"If that's a challenge, I accept."

"You know, you weren't the only one with a lot on your mind." Anne held both of Zeke's hands to her chest. "While you were gone, I worried, I rationalized, and I remembered. And do you know what memory came back first and strongest?"

Zeke shook her head.

"It was how wickedly my body reacts whenever you touch me." She stroked the side of Zeke's face with her fingertips caressing the warm soft skin. "I think what we have together is real and I'm willing to fight your demons and the devil himself in order to keep it."

"You have no idea what that means to me."

The room was dark except for the glow of the fireplace across the room. Anne sat Zeke down at the foot of the bed and pulled the tee shirt over her head. She stood looking at Zeke's naked body. Without saying a word, she stepped forward, straddled Zeke's legs, untied her own robe, and let it slip to the floor.

"I need to touch you so badly." Zeke slid her hands up Anne's thighs as she pressed her lips to her abdomen.

Anne swooned as Zeke ran the tip of her tongue very slowly up her belly and kissed each breast lovingly and thoroughly.

"Oh, God, yes."

Zeke's hands caressed each buttock then used her gentle fingers to explore, massage, and tease while she continued suckling each breast.

Anne's legs began to tremble as the burning desire filled her with a scorching need. Unable to contain it, she moaned deeply.

Zeke pulled her onto the bed and continued to

probe the throbbing between Anne's legs.

Anne pushed her hips against Zeke's hand slowly at first, then more urgently and vocally. "Oh yes," she cried as Zeke nibbled and kissed her breast.

"Tell me what you want," Zeke whispered.

The passionate dance excited both until finally, through clenched teeth, Anne said, "Harder."

Zeke obediently stroked her with practiced patience.

Anne writhed with the exquisite sensations. "Now, please—now."

"I thought you'd never ask." Zeke obliged her with fierce, loving passion, and pushed Anne to an explosive climax.

Anne collapsed on top of Zeke panting. Their bodies hot and wet. Their heaving chests synchronized as Anne's heart thundered through her ribs. Every nerve and every cell was alive and thrumming with electricity. Anne smiled. "Now, my love, it's your turn."

Intoxicated with her own fire, Anne greedily sucked Zeke's tongue into her mouth kissing her hard. Fingers traced the familiar body eliciting moans from Zeke when she rolled a nipple between her fingers. Anne stopped her mouth's assault and pulled back. "You're so beautiful," she whispered. With her passion mounting, Anne nipped Zeke's neck in several places before capturing a nipple and sucking it deep into her mouth.

The trembling body beneath her pitched and writhed with a keening sound. Her need was overpowering. Anne slowly slid her fingers and hungry mouth across Zeke's heaving chest and abdomen to each thigh, spreading them.

Zeke quivered, whimpered, and clutched the

headboard as Anne slowly teased and tortured her to the brink of ecstasy and with deliberate tenderness, pushed her over the brink. Zeke cried out, her back arched, and muscle spasms rippled across her body.

Then, it was over.

Anne watched as Zeke's body crumpled and she sobbed deeply releasing waves of sadness. Anne crawled closer to her side holding her very tightly. Drained and ecstatic she whispered very softly, "I adore you."

Chapter Eight

It was still early when Zeke awoke alone and she listened for signs of life. Hearing nothing, she pulled on her discarded tee shirt and checked the bathrooms. The house was eerily quiet. She quickly dressed and ran downstairs. This didn't seem to be the ideal start to their new life 'together'. Checking the garage, she found Anne's car gone. *She must have gone to the store.* Zeke remembered their conversation from the night before.

In the kitchen, she saw a note on the counter sticking out of a coffee mug.

Dear Zeke,
In all the Excitement ☺ last night,
I completely forgot that I had to work. ☹
Make yourself at home and call me when you get up.
Love, A

She smiled, and then set about making a fresh pot of coffee. Zeke carried a cup into the family room where the morning sun was blazing through the large east facing windows. She stood for a moment to take it all in. Other than the wall clock that was ticking and the refrigerator that was humming, there was complete silence. It felt strange and wonderful. Her body felt a little bruised but alive with excitement. She couldn't remember the last time she'd made love like a sex-starved teenager. And, she had certainly forgotten the therapeutic value. She felt reborn.

Zeke perched on the arm of the sofa; the view from the family room covered the east side of the property. The leaves on the eastern slope turned gold, and the sunlight glistened on the morning dew like tiny prisms. Anne's lot sloped down toward the highway that meandered through the gentle hills of the East Mountains. Most of the trees were conifers interspersed with a few oak and maple trees.

Two large copper bird feeders hanging over the deck were nearly empty and she made a mental note to add bird feed to a shopping list.

She sipped the savory coffee as she looked around. Even in the short time she'd stayed with Anne, this house had started to feel like home. She had a sense of belonging and safety. The comfortable leather side chair fit her long lean frame perfectly and propped her legs on the nearby ottoman.

Her mind wandered back as she closed her eyes. Ever since a drive-by accident four years earlier in DC, which took the life of her girlfriend, Zeke had chosen to live in hotels, rooming houses, B&B's and, lastly, under the El tracks in Chicago. *Rootless*. She had been alone and virtually homeless for much of her adult life except for that very brief lapse. Without attachments of any kind, Zeke was able to focus all of her energy and most of her time on her job. It made her an exceptional undercover agent but a lonely human being. That was her choice, then, but sitting in this warm inviting home felt like a new beginning, and although she felt good, prickles of fear edged her joy.

Zeke basked in the glow and warmth of the wavering sunlight as it fluttered across her closed eyes and the still fresh memory of their lovemaking. Defenses down, she sensed rather than felt a cold spot somewhere in her chest. *Doubt?* The tiniest red flag jerked her to attention. There was something else, something out there, and she couldn't name or put a face on it. She tried to block the squeaky cautionary voice in her head as she sipped her coffee.

A new chapter in her life beckoned and she knew with certainty that she and Anne were a good balance because her well-constructed defensive wall was crumbling. The siren call of love was irresistible. Zeke knew the adjustment would be difficult for both of them. Most of her co-workers were married—so it had to be possible to integrate work and family.

She got up to refill her coffee cup and looked around. A set of matched copper cookware hung over the island stovetop. The soapstone counter held a glass canister set with hand written labels. *That's so Anne.* When she opened the nearest cupboard, Zeke shook her head and smiled at the way the condiments lined up alphabetically. Even the plants in the window sat arranged by size. Zeke realized how much she didn't know about the extraordinary woman with whom she would be living.

Years as a highly trained observer allowed her to quickly assess a scene and commit the details to memory. After looking through the refrigerator and freezer, she moved through each kitchen cabinet analyzing the content for patterns. She routinely did this kind of exercise in new situations to stay sharp.

Zeke grabbed a pad of paper from the counter near the phone; she moved into the family room and wrote down what she remembered. Feeling more confident with what she could remember, she went back to check her results. She had missed the Dijon mustard and that the mayonnaise was Hellmann's. Not bad though, considering her head injury, PTSD, mood swings, and the recent blackout in Arizona, all of which had been discouraging.

Armed with confidence and energy, Zeke showered, dressed, backed her car out of the garage, and headed off to the grocery store. She called Anne en route but got her voicemail.

"Hi there, you are probably with a patient but I'm on my way to The Market and I wanted to see if there was anything you needed. Let me know."

✝

At that moment, Anne was trying hard to replace a Foley catheter for a confused elderly patient. *Damn textbooks.* Not everyone had the same anatomy and trying to locate that tiny opening in an eighty-seven year old woman with dementia, arthritis, and knee contractures was difficult at best.

Anne spoke gently and reassuringly to the poor woman, while the daughter held one knee and a flashlight. It was difficult to maintain a sterile field in the small, cluttered, overheated bedroom with perspiration clouding her vision. *At last, success.* She watched the clear tubing to be sure that she had correctly placed the catheter then inflated the small balloon to hold it in place.

"There, that should be good for another month. Let's get her into some pajama bottoms that will hopefully prevent her pulling at it."

"Thank you so much, I'm sorry that mother is so difficult. It seems that she gets so agitated whenever anyone has to do something for her." The daughter looked embarrassed.

"Please don't apologize. I'm sure I'd react the same way if I were confused and someone tried to catheterize me. In fact, I'm quite sure I would also be cursing."

They talked briefly while Anne charted notes then made her goodbyes and headed out to her car. The flashing cell phone indicated a message. As she listened, she smiled. Having a lover to come home to at night made the day go quicker. Anne could feel a flush spreading through her body which was certainly hormone related but not in a bad way. Menopause didn't seem to be affecting her libido.

Anne started the car and headed to her next patient. Her work with patients all day in nurse mode and then hearing Zeke's voice, made her remember the fainting episode in Arizona. She scribbled a note on the front of a folder to find out if syncope or petit mal seizures might be symptoms for head injuries or PTSD.

While Zeke was gone in Chicago, Anne researched PTSD. She was surprised to learn there was even a subcategory for Rape Trauma Syndrome. Unsure what Zeke discussed with the psychiatrist, Anne was reluctant to interfere but recognized some of the signs. Zeke had definitely lost weight and was not eating well—not to mention the nightmares and the startle reflex. That worried Anne. On the plus side, Zeke allowed herself to be touched, maybe that was because Anne was a woman and they had a special relationship. Men might pose more of a threat. That seemed clear from her overreaction to the couple in the park.

She turned into the first fast food place she found, ordered something to drink, then drove around the building to pick up per order.

"Thank you," she said to the elderly man who handed her the drink. She carefully merged her car back into a line of traffic and her mind went back into her thought process. Zeke rocked her world and it felt so good to have a passion that she felt had died, if it ever existed, awaken. Anne wanted to help Zeke in any way that she could.

She laughed when she sipped through the straw and noticed that the muscles in her jaw along with her tongue were tender. *Clearly I'm out of practice.*

As she recalled their second meeting on the hiking trail, Anne smiled. Poor Zeke sat on a log bloodied and bruised with a gun gripped in her hand. It might have been funny if the weapon hadn't been so frightening. But once she sat next to the injured woman to assess the injuries and touched beautiful, soft, brown skin, something inside her awakened. At the time, she didn't recognize the physical desire for what it was. But as she continued to care for Zeke, she began to notice the slight thrill she would feel with the thought of their physical proximity.

Then, the electricity between them ignited a desire that began to grow. When Zeke finally made the first move and kissed her softly and sensually a few days later, there were fireworks. Anne laughed as she remembered running from the room believing she might have actually been able to fly. No one had ever kissed her like that. And she had never in her life thought it could happen with a virtual stranger, especially not a woman.

The memory of that afternoon was enough to stir desire in her belly. *Could it really only have been a month ago?* She took another drink as a grin teased the corners of her lips.

Traffic eased as Anne headed west into one of the subdivisions. Anne fumbled with her Bluetooth headset then dialed Zeke's number.

"Cabot."

"Hi, Zeke, I'm returning your call."

"Hi, you. Glad you called. I missed you this morning. What are you doing?"

"Driving to my next patient and thinking about you, *fondly*."

"Hmm, pay attention to your driving," Zeke said.

"It ain't easy, girl."

"Do you need anything?"

"I sure do!"

"I mean from the store."

"No, not really."

"Well hurry home, I'm cooking for you."

"I can't wait."

"Me, too."

Anne smiled as she disconnected the call. A warm sensation grew inside and flowed to her arms and legs. Zeke's soft lilting drawl made her skin tingle. She still had three patients to visit as well as lab work to deliver. She was having trouble focusing. Her mind and body obsessed with thoughts of the beautiful woman with the soft lips and loving hands.

†

Zeke put away all the groceries, stuck the folded grocery bags in the pantry, and took a bottle of water from the refrigerator. She retrieved her laptop from the hall and set it up on the large ottoman in front of a comfortable armchair in the library.

Before sitting, she stretched her back and hamstrings. The stiffness and muscle aches were new and in spite of her morning exercise routine, she continued to have discomfort on most days. "Guess middle age is creepin' up on me."

For several days, her laptop sat unused so she wasn't surprised to find so many emails. The first was from Dr. Nilsson providing the name of a colleague at the University of New Mexico, a Dr. Robin Taylor. She was willing to forward her notes if Zeke sent her permission. Zeke noted the name, phone number, and replied with permission and her gratitude.

The next message was from Special Agent Hartbrooke with the preliminary approval of transfer to the Albuquerque office and the name of her new supervisor, Angela de la Hoya. *Excellent. It will be a nice surprise for Anne.* Zeke felt a little excited thinking about returning to work in another month.

Zeke skimmed through several notes from colleagues and her family wondering how she was enjoying her 'vacation' and if she was 'bored by all of the 'lying around.' *Ha.* There was an inquiry from Agent Mike Donovan in the New Mexico Field office, asking her to call him. *He must have gotten a call from Frank Hartbrooke.*

It was almost two p.m. when Zeke finished setting up appointments with Dr. Taylor and her new supervisor both on Thursday.

She closed the laptop and headed to the kitchen to start making the spicy vodka cream sauce for the penne pasta. After washing her hands, Zeke remembered she hadn't eaten all day and was a little hungry; she threw some ham on a hard roll and munched as she rooted through drawers pulling out various implements, bowls, and seasonings. The variety of ingredients on the counter made her smile. Zeke decided that having a kitchen to create a meal was fun, especially as the kitchen became more familiar.

It had been so long since she had shared her life and a home with someone. *Home.* Zeke looked forward to making a home with Anne and sharing all of the mundane daily activities that people do when they blend two separate lives.

It felt comfortable living in a safe place instead of living hand to mouth as she had undercover in Chicago. She smiled as she realized it had been over twenty-four hours since she had experienced any flashbacks. *Maybe Sandra was right, healing might actually happen.* Anne was certainly good medicine for her.

Zeke found herself fantasizing about the incredibly gentle spirit that concealed a hot-blooded woman. She wilted with Anne's powerful hunger and passion, but at the same time, there was an intense desire to please Anne. It had always been difficult for her to talk about feelings. It was easier to show her. Zeke had never met anyone quite as exciting as a lover or as stable and grounded a professional. She was a mature woman with an adult appetite and a generous spirit. Zeke felt lucky.

She added the vodka to the cream sauce and lowered the heat to let it simmer.

†

Anne finished with her last patient and hurried to deliver blood samples to the lab before it closed. She stopped only briefly to grab a small bouquet of fresh flowers then threaded her way through the rush hour traffic in downtown Albuquerque. She reached Tijeras Canyon just as the sun dipped below the west mesa painting the sky pink and orange in her rearview mirror.

As she entered the house from the garage, Anne smelled a fragrant tangy scent emanating from her kitchen, which led her to a couple of large pots steaming on the stove.

Zeke was at the sink washing vegetables.

"Hi, Hon, I'm home, and boy, does it smell good." Anne wrapped her arms tightly around Zeke's waist.

"It'll be ready in about twenty minutes, okay?"

"Perfect, that'll give me time to take care of the horses." Anne jogged up stairs to change her clothes.

By the time she returned from feeding the horses, she could see candles lit in the dining room. Zeke had set the table with everything she could find, linens, china and crystal and the flowers Anne had left on the counter.

Zeke pulled out a chair. "Madam." Once Anne was sitting, she served a tantalizing penne pasta with vodka cream sauce, spinach salad, baked garlic parmesan bread, accompanied by a very smooth Cab-Sav from South America.

Anne heard her stomach growl as the different aromas filled her nose. She was suddenly ravenous with hunger. "I can't remember the last time I smelled such a heavenly combination." She savored the first bite and groaned. "This is divine. I never would've pegged you for gourmet cook."

"Oh, I wouldn't go quite that far. There are two or three recipes that I've mastered, but I am far from gourmet."

Anne glanced across the table at Zeke's smiling face glowing from the candlelight. "Thank you. This was really sweet."

The remainder of the dinner conversation was light. Anne described her day, and then Zeke told her about her conversations and the appointments she'd made.

"I have another surprise for you, Annie."

"Really?"

"Yeah, I got an e-mail today that confirmed my transfer request."

Anne looked up as her fork clanged against her plate. "A transfer?"

"I didn't want to say anything until it was confirmed, but I asked to be transferred to the Albuquerque Field office."

"That's wonderful. I was really hoping that you would, but I didn't want to jinx it. Oh, Zeke, I'm so happy." Anne raised both arms in the air and clapped her hands.

"I'll start December first, but I'll probably meet with my new boss before then."

"Speaking of work," Anne said, "I almost forgot. The oddest thing happened today. Two or three times I thought I saw the same car behind me, you know, as if he was following me. Then it would disappear. But it happened in Albuquerque and Rio Rancho, so I doubt it was the same car."

"You don't think it was your ex, Andrew, do you?" asked Zeke.

"No. I'd know that big gaudy Mercedes anywhere."

"Do you remember what kind of car it was?"

"It was dark blue or grey, not sure. It had tinted windows so I couldn't see who was driving. But I was in different neighborhoods around the city, so it sure seemed like a funny coincidence to me."

"Huh, tell me if you see the car again and try to see the plate number." Zeke stood up and paused, then cleared the dinner plates.

Chapter Nine

Tuesday dawned cold and ominous. November had made its entrance. Low hanging velvet gray clouds skidded across the mountains on their journey east. October had been unseasonably mild, and Zeke watched with interest as leaden streaks raced across the sky through their bedroom window. She'd grown accustomed to the boundless blue skies and sunshine.

Zeke pulled the covers up around her ears, rolled onto her side, and bunched the pillow a little closer. Anne made her promise to stay in bed for a while so why not. It was warm and smelled sweetly of laundry soap and the lingering scent of Anne's perfume. She closed her eyes briefly and savored the memory of sleeping wrapped around Anne's body. The nightmares still visited but were less frightening with Anne beside her.

The sound of morning activity gradually intruded. She could hear Anne moving around the kitchen and the radio playing in the background. Even though Anne only worked two days a week as a Home Health nurse, her job required a significant amount of paperwork. Given the amount of time and energy devoted to filling out forms, Zeke was surprised there was any time left to treat sick people. Anne rarely complained and she was able to do most of it from home on her laptop computer. From her own personal experience, the patients who benefited from Anne's care were pretty darn lucky. Her nurse was the best.

Zeke glanced at the clock and knew she needed to

call Donovan so she reluctantly crawled out of bed. After a welcome trip to the bathroom, Zeke made the bed and set about her morning routine of calisthenics. Thanks to her father's rigid military routine, she had followed his example and completed the same exercises every morning for the past thirty years. The sit-ups, pushups, jumping jacks, and stretches lasted only fifteen to twenty minutes but served their purpose.

The smell of coffee wafted upstairs tempting her, but Zeke resisted so she could call Donovan and check that off her list. She closed the door and dialed her cell phone.

"Donovan."

"Hi, Mike. It's Zeke Cabot returning your call."

"Hey there, welcome back. How was the trip to Chicago? Did you sort out the paperwork?"

Zeke sat down in a chair next to the window. "I hope so. Lord knows we put in enough hours. It turns out the Hussein brothers had numerous business dealings including a couple of offshore accounts. I left it in the capable hands of the analysts, since white collar is not my specialty."

"Listen, the reason I wanted to talk to you is that I did a little more background work. We may have additional international connections with Mubarak, his cousins in Phoenix, and their connection to the Hussein brothers. The reason our office decided to follow up is the probable drug connections. I dug a little deeper into this Mubarak character and it became more convoluted the deeper I went."

Zeke listened as her counterpart shuffled papers and tapped on his keyboard.

"After Phoenix FBI visited him following your attack, his wife sent a message to Beirut, possibly to Hassan, regarding your identity and possible location.

Evidently, Mubarak has been sharing information with the Hussein brothers for years. We're still sorting details on Hassan's network, but in addition to his regular imports, there is considerable suspicion about drugs and money laundering, especially Middle Eastern money."

"I guess I'm not surprised. Sorry we didn't check a little further, but we were trying so hard to nail the doctor for murder and he was slippery." Zeke wished she had taken the time to look at the file that Hartbrooke had given her. "I received a file when I was in Chicago but haven't opened it. My former partner tagged it for me before he died, and if it has anything helpful I will certainly let you know. You should probably let Hartbrooke know what you found."

"Will do."

"Mike, I thought I should let you know that I requested a transfer to Albuquerque."

"That's great. We could really use the help, especially with the drug problem. Do you have any idea when that might happen?"

He sounded genuinely excited.

"Probably December first, because I still have some vacation time to use. I have a preliminary meeting with Special Agent in Charge de la Hoya, on Thursday. Do you think she'll want to put me on drug detail?"

"Maybe. We really could use someone with your experience. New Mexico covers over one-hundred-twenty-one million square miles with a population of two million. Because of the small population, it doesn't seem to warrant the federal dollars we really need, even though it's a border state. Whenever possible, we try to work with the other agencies.

They both laughed a little knowing how difficult it was for different Agencies to work together.

"Honestly, Zeke, it's frustrating. There's a lot of contraband that comes across that border, and we miss most of it. We need all the help we can get. I would sure like to work with you."

"I'd enjoy that too. I guess we'll have to wait and see. In the meantime, I'll look through that file and see what I can find out."

"Appreciate that. Take care."

Zeke disconnected and stared at the display on her smart phone. The picture was of the Gulf coast shoreline, her home. Some of the conversations from her last case replayed in her mind. She tried to recollect any mention of drug or contraband connections without luck. She'd need to review her notes and the mysterious file folder from Detective Shapiro.

†

Anne hung up after getting the call from the lab and charted lab values for Mr. Garcia, so the special program on her computer could calculate his next dose of heart medication. She picked up her cell phone and dialed his number.

"Hello."

"Good morning, Mrs. Garcia, this is Anne, the Home Health nurse. I wanted you to know that your husband's blood test showed improvement, so you only have to give him one pill. He only needs the 4 mg pill."

"Is that the blue one?"

"Yes, just give him that one pill along with his other meds and one of the nurses will be over to draw his blood in a little while."

"Okay, I will do that. Gracias."

Anne finished writing the entry from her visit the day before. The stiffness in her neck began to bother

her and she rolled her shoulders. A little more coffee couldn't hurt. She walked around the cook top island to the coffee maker. She could hear Zeke talking to someone upstairs but couldn't make out any of the words. A smile began as she stirred sweetener into her coffee. It was nice having someone in the house. She glanced at the ceiling hearing Zeke laugh and thought about the wonderful meal Zeke had prepared her the night before. The more she learned about this mysterious woman the more intriguing she became. Each day helped to peel away another layer of Zeke's character.

Last night uncovered a more domestic Zeke. Anne shook her head. An enigmatic federal agent involved in some very dangerous work concealed many layers, each more intriguing than the last. But just below the surface, anxiety nibbled at her consciousness as she thought about the danger surrounding Zeke's job.

Federal law enforcement types—like FBI, CIA or half a dozen others—were always the stuff of fiction. Nameless—faceless—mysterious. Anne remembered the number of local police officers when she worked in the hospital and they had a very cordial, symbiotic relationship with medical people. *This is going to be an interesting ride.*

Anne finished her coffee and rinsed her cup. Soon she found herself rearranging dishes in the dishwasher and washing the tops of her canisters as her mind wandered freely from one topic to the next.

Most of the time, Zeke's tenderness and affection were enough to keep lingering fears at bay. But sometimes out of nowhere, Anne remembered the two men and the assault—that memory made her stomach clench. Nurses were not squeamish and were accustomed to treating victims of crime. That crime had been different because it was very personal. When that fear crept into her stomach, Anne feared the possibility of another assault. Being afraid was something new. It bothered her when she told Zeke that someone might be following her—Zeke seemed unconcerned.

Anne moved into the family room and straightened up the magazines on the coffee table and refolded woolen throws on the couch. The conversation upstairs sounded cordial. Certainly, Zeke was entitled to make private phone calls; still the mysterious content of those conversations worried her.

"Enough fretting. You've got work to finish." She returned to her charting. Anne had finished two more notes on the computer when Zeke appeared in the doorway looking sharp. Straight leg jeans and a royal blue V-neck sweater fit her lean frame perfectly. Her wavy hair nearly reached her collar with one curl hanging irresistibly over her forehead. Anne swallowed hard then smiled.

"Well, good morning lazy bones," Anne grinned.

"Good morning, Miss Anne, it looks like you've been busy." Zeke moved around the breakfast table and placed a warm hand on the back of Anne's neck before pressing her lips with a soft kiss.

An electric jolt coursed through Anne's body, which responded on its own. Small muscles along the nerve pathway twitched as Anne arched up for more.

Zeke kissed her again once, twice then slowly withdrew. "That's a nice way to start the day."

"I'll say." Anne felt the artery in her neck pulsing. "Would you like some breakfast?"

"I think I'll just have some coffee right now. I'd like to run over to that shop next to The Market for a haircut. Their sign invited walk-ins." Zeke pulled an insulated travel cup out of the cupboard and poured coffee.

Anne chewed the end of her pen, and watched Zeke move with a cat-like grace about the kitchen with more than passing interest. The long legs and firm derriere encased in those jeans was distracting her from her work.

"Okay. I'm almost finished then I have some things to work on in the barn."

"If you wait till I get back, I'll help you. I shouldn't be too long." Zeke tightened the lid on her cup.

"Don't worry about it, nothing major. You take your time."

Zeke scooped up her wallet, keys and sunglasses and looked around for anything she might have forgotten. She leaned one hand on the doorjamb. "You know, today might be a good day to do something about my leased car."

"Isn't your appointment at the FBI Office on Thursday?"

Zeke smacked her forehead with the heel of her hand. "Of course, no need to make two trips into town I guess. I'm sure they won't mind if I keep the agency car a couple of more days. See you later."

Anne watched as her lover clipped a badge to her waist then attached the holster and gun she had pulled from the drawer in the sideboard. A band tightened around her chest. *Will I feel this scared every day when she does that?*

†

Anne's car was gone when Zeke arrived so she parked near the garage. Side trips to the bookstore and a bakery had taken longer than she planned. She reached for the bestseller and a bag of freshly baked chocolate chip cookies she'd purchased then looked around for the bottle of conditioner the stylist had sold her. It seemed harder to keep track of her belongings lately, but Zeke assumed it had to do with moving into a new place.

After leaving the cookies on the kitchen counter, she went upstairs to change. Even though they used a plastic drape and tissue around her neck, it felt like there was clipped hair everywhere, and she couldn't wait to change her clothes.

When she reached the top of the stairs, something looked different. On the large balcony style landing, the furniture, a large area rug, a brass floor lamp, and a nice armchair where re-arranged and her computer along with her locked briefcase were in the center of the long L-shaped mahogany desk. She picked up the note on top of her laptop.

Hope this isn't presumptuous—thought you might like a place to work, Annie.

Once again, the reality of a relationship with another person was like a splash of cold water in the face. Zeke bristled, because it was, in fact, 'presumptuous'. However, it was Anne's house.

They probably needed to sit down and set up some rules and boundaries together. Zeke's compartment-alization issues had evidently extended far beyond her psyche. She cherished her privacy and personal space. Knowing they were both giving up some of their privacy didn't seem to ease the discomfort.

After toweling off her neck and shoulders then changing into her favorite Southern Miss sweatshirt, the newly 'coupled' agent sat down at the beautiful desk. She spun around in the handsome leather chair and proceeded to set up her laptop using the pre-drilled openings that concealed the cords. It was a good location with great light and a nice view of the family room and the large east facing windows. It was a comfortable workspace. She suddenly was touched with Annie's thoughtfulness. She smiled. "Okay, maybe this won't be so bad, I can get used to this."

†

When Anne arrived home around two, she found Zeke seated at her new desk making notes and reading reports from several open file folders.

Zeke stopped and turned. "Hi there, beautiful."

"Hi, you." She quickly hung up the dry cleaning in the master bedroom then returned to the landing and plopped into the armchair near the window. "That's some haircut. I like it." Anne smiled at her. "I figured you must have had some other errands you needed to do so I went ahead without you on the barn chores after I set this up, then left to run some of my own errands."

Zeke spun the chair to face her. "Uh, yeah. I stopped at the bookstore and bakery. I had no idea how long I was gone. I'm sorry." She waved her hand across the desk. "This is really awesome. I can't believe you did all this in the time I was gone. It's really perfect. Thank you."

Anne felt pleased with her surprise. "I'm glad you like it. I thought about it for a while but wasn't sure you'd like it. Andrew used it for an office, and after he left, I dismantled it so I wouldn't have to think about him. It is a nice space to work."

"Don't you want to use it?"

"No, I much prefer the kitchen."

"Okay. And your timing is perfect. Because after talking to Mike Donovan this morning, I promised to review my case notes. As you can see, I clearly needed a place to spread them out."

Case notes? "Do you have something new to work on?" Anne asked. *I thought that the transfer had just gone through and she's already working? So much for another month together.*

"Mike filled me in on some of the problems they encounter in New Mexico. He was curious about whether or not my last case had any connections." Zeke stretched her legs out and folded her arms behind her head. "Special Agent in Charge Hartbrooke gave me some notes when I was in Chicago. The detective I worked with—the one killed in a hit and run accident—sent them to me at the Chicago office. I can only assume that he found something and thought I should see it. It could be relevant or it might be nothing. Since he went to the trouble to make sure I got it, I felt like I should go through the notes." She shrugged.

"I was just worried they had put you to work already and we wouldn't have as much time together."

"Don't worry, darlin', we'll have lots of time together." Zeke flashed an irresistible smile.

"Hey, are you flirting with me, Special Agent Cabot?"

"Yes, ma'am, I am, because the way those slacks and turtleneck hug your body, I'm getting a little jealous."

Anne felt heat bloom in her cheeks. "Why, thank you. I might add that someone did an especially good job on your hair. It's a lot shorter but flattering. It makes those gorgeous brown eyes glow."

Zeke rolled her chair closer, leaned forward, and stood. "I'm really glad you're home."

The soft moist lips so close to her face drew Anne like a magnet. When they touched, she felt the electric charge to her core. She closed her eyes as Zeke's hands caressed the sides of her face and yielded to the invitation on her lips.

Chapter Ten

Thursday morning Anne came downstairs dressed for work wearing a set of navy blue scrubs, a white cardigan sweater, and a pair of white Nike's with a stethoscope draped around her neck. To Zeke's adoring eye, she looked like the quintessential poster of a beautiful and alluring professional nurse. It triggered good and bad memories of being in the care of the wonderful nurse recently.

Anne glanced at the plate on the counter and Zeke's breakfast attempt. "This is sweet of you." She gave Zeke a warm good morning kiss.

"I made you an egg salad sandwich, a cup of applesauce, and some cookies, if you want it." Zeke held up a paper bag.

Anne laughed and pulled her forward by the hand to kiss her again. "If you keep doing such nice things— I may never get to work." Anne grabbed her travel cup of coffee, the lunch sack, the toasted bagel and headed out to her car.

Zeke waved and rubbed her hand across her chest. With every passing day, the heavy chain protecting her heart weakened. She glanced at the kitchen clock then headed upstairs to shower and dress for her two appointments in town. She needed to leave early since she was unfamiliar with the University of New Mexico and the campus buildings.

†

Dr. Robin Taylor was on the faculty of both the University and the Hospital. Her office was located in a house just east of the hospital off Lomas Blvd. The home housed two other doctors and had a small waiting area, which was empty. At ten a.m., a young woman came in and introduced herself as Dr. Taylor. She was short, maybe five foot two, slender, with short, dark brown hair, and intense brown eyes.

Zeke, expecting someone older and not quite as attractive, jumped to her feet.

The petite woman was energetic. She reached forward taking Zeke's hand firmly and asked in a very businesslike manner, "Are you, Zeke Cabot?"

"Yes, how do you do?" Zeke was quickly ushered into a room that might once have been a study. Dark wood trim with white plaster walls and an antique ceiling fixture made the room seem old and familiar.

The wooden furniture was old institutional style, but the room contained numerous bright, colorful fabrics on pillows, throws, and wall hangings that looked to be Guatemalan. The space was small but comfortable.

"Please sit down." Dr. Taylor pointed to a wooden rocker next to the east-facing window and across from a large cluttered desk, where she sat. "I have scheduled you for an hour and a half since it is our first session— but you may not need to use all that unless we run long."

"That's fine." Zeke felt intimidated by this slight but powerful presence.

Dr. Taylor began by opening a folder from her desk. "I reviewed Dr. Nilsson's very thorough notes." She paused and put down the folder. "It might help you feel more comfortable to know that Dr. Nilsson and I completed a fellowship together. We spent the summer in El Salvador ten years ago working with women who were victims of the military junta. Because of my background, she thought that you and I would be able to work together. Is there anything you'd like to ask before we start?"

"I don't think so," stammered Zeke. This new therapist exuded an assertive confidence and was totally unlike Dr. Nilsson's calm nurturing manner. It wasn't a bad thing, but Zeke felt off balance and guarded.

Dr. Taylor crossed her legs and leaned back in her chair so the sun reflected across her lap. Her eyes narrowed as she focused on Zeke and lowered her voice. "Zeke, why don't you tell me what you think we should work on."

Flashback. Powerless. Vulnerable. Zeke closed her eyes. "I want to have control of my life again."

The next thirty minutes were consumed with Zeke's detached retelling of the collateral damage from the assault nearly three weeks earlier and the toll it exacted on her self esteem, professional skills, and most important of all, her personal relationship. Zeke described the recurring nightmares and flashbacks as well as her loss of appetite. She stopped, took a deep breath, and put her head down. Depleted—as though she had run a mile.

"How do you feel right now?"

"Actually, I feel a little shaky and drained."

"Would you like some water?" Dr. Taylor handed her a plastic bottle from the end table.

"Thank you." She gulped several swallows.

"Have you been able to talk about this assault with anyone else?"

"Yes, I talked with a couple of friends in Chicago, and of course, Dr. Nilsson. I also went to Flagstaff to meet with a former Agent who was—was raped."

"That word still holds a charge for you, doesn't it?"

"I guess so." Zeke realized that every time she heard the word, her insides seized up painfully.

"If you are willing, I would like you to recall that day and I'd like you describe to me what happened to you from an emotional point of view, specifically how you felt. Can you do that? If it becomes painful, I want you to breathe and keep talking."

Zeke's stomach lurched. She took a deep breath and closed her eyes remembering the first moment she laid eyes on the beautiful stranger. She began by sharing Anne and her chance meetings followed by the embarrassing snake incident on the trail.

"We enjoyed some magical days together. Both of us were aware of the powerful attraction. We spent time together trying not to jump into anything prematurely, but finally decided we needed a little get-away to get to know each other. When we got to Taos, well, it was just astonishing." Zeke blushed at the memory of their lovemaking and passion.

"On Saturday we toured around the Enchanted Circle, sightseeing, taking pictures, and getting comfortable with each other." Zeke stiffened as the icy memories intruded. "I had a feeling something was off. I had received warnings from the office about some interest in my whereabouts, but my enthusiasm and hormones were overriding my natural warning system." She stopped. Her pulse rate increased, and she felt perspiration on the back of her neck. Was 'that' the problem? Had she screwed up? Zeke took a deep breath. "After lunch we stopped to check out a campground which was isolated and somewhat romantic. We started kissing and I was distracted." She blushed and watched Dr. Taylor make a note. It was embarrassing but she needed to say it. "I felt relaxed and started getting aroused. Metal banging on the window jolted me back and I found myself staring into the barrel of a gun. I struggled to organize my thoughts and figure out what was happening; how in the hell I was taken by surprise; and how to protect Anne."

Zeke trembled as the words spilled out of her mouth "I had a weapon under the seat but no way to get it. I told Anne to do what they said." She paused when her voice cracked then took deep breaths. "They got us out of the car and told me who they were looking for and I told them what I knew—they didn't believe me." Zeke's chest burned and it was hard to breathe, she looked up at Dr. Taylor.

"You're all right. Go on."

"That's when I lost it and got scared. They were in control—they were holding a gun to Anne's head. The younger guy hit me several times then threw me on the ground." Zeke struggled to breathe slowly while tears ran down her face. "I woke up on the ground with Anne holding my head. It was awful. I felt dirty, violated, scared, and weak." The only sound that Zeke could hear for several minutes was the clock on the wall and her own ragged breathing.

"What happened next?" asked the soft voice across from her.

"Anne was there, holding my hand and reassuring me."

"And have you both been able to talk about this since then?"

"Well, some. We haven't really talked about that day but more about what to do now. She was the one who suggested counseling."

"Why do you think she suggested it?"

"Because I was having trouble connecting or being present sometimes, and she felt too close to be objective."

"She was right. How has she treated you since then? Has there been any strain or distance?"

"No, she's been really supportive and patient. I think she knows what's going on but doesn't want to push me."

"What is the major concern you have right now, today?"

"I'm lucky to have found this woman, and I really want to be able to build a life with her. The question right now is whether I can support her and do my job— or even if I will be able to do my job."

"All right. We have several things to explore. I would like you to talk to your partner as honestly as possible and try to explain your feelings about the assault. That means, letting her know that a small part of you blames her. Do you understand that?"

Zeke shook her head. "But I don't blame her."

"Do you think you would have handled that whole episode differently if you had been alone?"

"Well sure. I would've been more alert. I wouldn't have been caught unarmed, and I would've taken control of the situation first."

Dr. Taylor raised her eyebrows in an 'as I said' expression. "Do you see?"

Zeke started to shake her head as a light flashed in her brain. She dropped her head back. "I blame her because I had to defend her and I couldn't do it because she distracted me. That's not fair—"

"And it's certainly a lot more complex. However, as long as you harbor the possibility for blame, it will be a wedge between you. You need to decide how much her presence and its distraction contributed to your assault and injury and whether there's a possibility it will continue to impact your work in a job where you are frequently exposed to danger."

Dr. Taylor looked at her watch then walked over to her desk. "I'd like to see you again next week, would this time work well?"

Zeke nodded. "That's fine. I'll check and let you know if it isn't."

"You did some good work today. This isn't easy. But I believe the more you talk about these things, the less power they will have over you."

†

Zeke thought about Dr. Taylor's last comment as she chewed her sandwich. It never occurred to her that her relationship and her job might intersect, and not in a good way. Then she thought about how easily someone found her. She made a mental note to review Agent Adams report from the attack. It might give her some clue about why a stranger had ambushed her so easily.

The last job in Chicago kept her deep undercover for months and she had only been in New Mexico a short time. Only a handful of people knew her approximate destination. So who leaked the information? It might be something to explore with her new boss. She glanced at the clock on the dashboard— she would be meeting her new boss very soon.

Zeke bagged up her trash and finished her soda. After locking the car, she walked across the street to a local bookstore. The clerk helped her find a copy of a regional guide for one-day excursions as well as a copy of the Real Estate Weekly. She still had vacation time left and she wanted to enjoy it as much time as possible

†

The FBI regional office was located north of Albuquerque and east of Interstate 25, close to downtown but in a less congested area. Since she had already met Agent Mike Donovan shortly after she landed in New Mexico the first time, Zeke was familiar with the building. She parked in the visitor lot, produced her ID at the guardhouse, and then followed the uniformed escort to the front desk where the receptionist phoned to announce her arrival.

Butterflies started in her stomach and the back of her shirt felt sticky. The x-ray security procedures didn't bother her, but this time she was meeting with her new boss.

The receptionist provided her with directions and buzzed her in the main door. Zeke stepped off the elevator and walked to the first door on her left which was the office of Special Agent in Charge, Angela de la Hoya. A dark haired Hispanic woman sat concentrating on her computer. Zeke wasn't sure whether to interrupt and tapped lightly on the doorframe.

"Special Agent Cabot, please come in and have a seat." Her new boss indicated a chair in front of her desk. She stood up and leaned over her desk extending her hand.

To Zeke she looked to be five foot six, with a nice figure, dark brown eyes, and a firm handshake. A gray pantsuit was expensive but worn. "Thank you, ma'am, I'm glad you could see me today."

"I was surprised but pleased when Agent Hartbrooke called me and told me you requested a transfer. I was a little worried that your first experience here was less than favorable, but maybe our beautiful state won you over."

"It was a combination of things. I've been with the Chicago office for several years and was due to transfer by the first of the year. It's also true that in the short amount of time I've been here, I've become one of the enchanted." Zeke unbuttoned her jacket and crossed her legs. The conversation flowed easier than she thought it would. "I've spent most of my career in large cities like Chicago, Washington, New York, and Atlanta. Albuquerque feels like a good fit."

Agent de la Hoya opened a file folder and paged through the contents. "I don't suppose I need to tell you your record is impressive Agent Cabot. You have received outstanding evaluations and several commendations. I can understand why Frank Hartbrooke was reluctant to let you go." She smiled for the first time.

Zeke felt her neck and face flushing with the compliment. Agent Hartbrooke treated her well and she knew he was fond of her. She felt a twinge of sadness when she thought of leaving him behind, but she could no longer work in Chicago—it held too many memories.

"Thank you, ma'am."

Agent de la Hoya closed the file, leaned back, and tented her fingers in front of her. "Is there anything you'd like to know about this office?"

Zeke hadn't really thought about it. "Well, as you know, I've worked with Agent Donovan on a couple of occasions, so I know a little about the office. I guess I'd like to know where you think I can serve best."

"You offer some excellent skills, especially your undercover talent. We have a unique situation in New Mexico because it's a large, mostly rural state with three or four primary cities. We are also one of the four southern border states. I'm sure you know how much trouble that brings us. The caseloads mostly consist of drug smuggling, gang activity, bank robberies, white-collar crime, and drugs. Just recently, we added a cyber crime division. A major area of concern is the security of the two national labs—Sandia and Los Alamos."

"That sounds like an awful lot to cover for a relatively small office."

"We have a number of smaller regional offices to share the work."

"You must have a pretty diverse staff."

Agent de la Hoya chuckled and shook her head. "Not as diverse as I'd like, but I am thrilled to welcome another woman, especially a woman of color to the team. The predominance of Hispanic and Native Americans in New Mexico makes it difficult for Anglo agents to infiltrate and gain trust."

Zeke realized, not for the first time, that her coloring could easily be mistaken for African American, Hispanic, or other mixed races. It had been beneficial to her on many occasions.

"Would you like to meet some of the other team members?"

"That would be great. I really like Mike, he's been incredibly helpful."

"Before I introduce you around, I would like to ask a favor." Agent de la Hoya came out from behind her desk and sat in a club chair next to Zeke. "I know you are still on medical leave and won't officially start for a few weeks. I called Agent Hartbrooke and asked if I could borrow you for a few hours—if you were agreeable. I'm in a bind and we have a rare opportunity tomorrow night. One of our Hispanic agents infiltrated a small cartel as a dealer. Tomorrow night they're celebrating the dealer's birthday and our agent garnered an invite. He'd be more credible if he brought an attractive woman with him. Since you are an unknown, it would be safer. And with your experience we'd have a much better chance at making a connection."

Zeke could feel her stomach tighten. The pounding started in her head. "Let me think about it, if I can." *Am I ready to jump back in and go undercover?* Everything inside of her screamed, 'no'.

"Of course, that's fine. It's just an idea, and you're not under any obligation. Let's go meet some of the folks."

Agent de la Hoya introduced her around the office as, Special Agent Zeke Cabot, the transfer from Chicago who helped to close the Danriga case on the 'homeless murders'.

There were smiles and handshakes, but Zeke could feel eyes watching her and twice heard whispered comments using the words 'gay' and 'dyke'. *Here we go again.* Although it was easier after fifteen years of service and a good record, it was annoying to have to deal with the petty bullshit.

They finished the tour at the office of Special Agent Gary Burton, who, according to Agent de la Hoya, had recently transferred in from the West Coast because of his experience with gangs. He was gracious and polite and seemed genuinely happy to have a new female agent in the office.

"I've just asked Agent Cabot if she would consider a special assignment before her start date." Agent de la Hoya smiled at Zeke.

Feeling a little cornered by the attention, Zeke's mind began swirling like a vortex—words and phrases tumbled over one another too quickly to grasp. She wanted to hit the pause button and make it stop. She looked at the other two agents standing in the room and she felt like she was looking down from the two-story building. They were talking to each other and hadn't noticed that Zeke was not part of their conversation.

She closed her eyes and tried to focus. *I'm all right nothing's going to happen.* When the quivering inside of her stopped, she reluctantly agreed to take the assignment for just one night. *It might be a good thing.* Maybe the trial by fire would help make her decision about her future. After all, if she came unglued now, at least she was off the clock and could withdraw her transfer request. She agreed to report in around five o'clock on Friday afternoon and, with luck, be finished with the assignment and on her way home within a few hours.

After touring the facility, Zeke climbed into her borrowed agency car with relief and turned east toward home. Just before she was ready to leave, she asked Agent de la Hoya about the status of her car. Zeke's leased car confiscated for evidence after the assault still wasn't ready, according to de la Hoya, so the trade would have to wait.

By the time she hit the canyon, Zeke began to have second thoughts about the request to help. On the upside, it would be an easy job and a chance to prove that she was a team player. Her stomach began to churn and the muscles in her shoulders tightened. Just thinking about going undercover again with unknown teammates made her increasingly anxious. She didn't know any of the new team well enough to know whom she could trust. Donovan was the only one she had talked to and he wouldn't be there. *Crap. Suck it up, Cabot, it's just a few hours, and it's a goddamn birthday party.*

†

Anne's car was right in front of her as she pulled up to the community entrance gate and she waved as

Anne punched in the security code. They both drove up to the house.

"You're home early." Zeke helped Anne unload the car.

"I planned it this way so I could have more time with you." Anne leaned forward and kissed her warmly.

Just one kiss and Zeke could feel her shoulders began to soften.

While Anne changed clothes then cared for her horses, Zeke slipped into a pair of jeans and a tee shirt and checked the refrigerator to see what might be available for dinner. There were some chicken breasts and broccoli so she was sure she could figure something out. In the meantime, she pulled out a bottle of white wine and removed the cork. She was waiting on the couch when Anne returned from the barn.

After washing the barn dust off, Anne joined Zeke on the couch. "Now tell me how your meetings went."

Zeke scooted down and crossed her ankles on the nearby coffee table.

"Dr. Taylor seems pretty nice. She's more intense than Dr. Nilsson is, but I think she's good. Fortunately she already had notes so I didn't have to go over some stuff again." She took a swallow of her wine and focused her attention on the front door at the end of the hallway. "But she did want me to recount the whole incident from the Columbine campground."

Anne shifted and put her arm around Zeke shoulders. "Was it hard?"

"Yeah. It always is."

"I'm sorry, baby."

Zeke patted her leg drawing strength from Anne's presence. "I'll see her again, and I'm sure it'll get easier."

Anne stroked Zeke's face. "I'm really glad you're

doing this. It may take awhile, but I think in the long run it will really help."

"I hope so. Most of the time I feel like I'm getting better but, you know, it never goes away completely." She caressed the fingers of Anne's hand.

"I know, baby, you still have nightmares, but they'll go away someday."

Zeke sat up and cleared her throat. She had to change the topic. It wasn't the time to talk about her anger and she knew Anne would press to hear more. Zeke didn't know how to describe her feelings without sounding accusing and she didn't want Anne to feel guilty.

"I just barely had time for lunch before I had to meet with Special Agent Angela de la Hoya." Zeke proceeded to describe her visit to the FBI office, her new coworkers, and her new boss. "She kinda blindsided me when she asked if I would be willing to work a few hours tomorrow night on an undercover operation. I'm not sure if I'm ready but felt it would be a good opportunity to show that I was a team player."

"Will it be dangerous?" Anne asked.

"No, I'll just be playing the girlfriend to one of the guys trying to make some drug connections. It'll be a meet and greet that shouldn't take more than a few hours. Why don't we make dinner?"

"Okay, if you say so." Anne stood. "I'm starved. What do you have in mind?"

Zeke prepared the chicken, and began chopping vegetables.

"By the way, did you think to mention the petit mal seizure you had in Arizona when you talked to Dr. Taylor?" Anne asked.

"No. I completely forgot about it." That much was true. Zeke's private nature and reluctance to share information prevented her from disclosing most things. Therapy might prove useful—she couldn't go on the way she had. But, opening up to a stranger would always be like pulling teeth to Zeke. She hated revealing anything about her personal life. Even trusting Anne after the hiking accident had taken an enormous effort, and even that wasn't a hundred percent trust. No one had ever gained full disclosure.

Chapter Eleven

Late Friday afternoon, Zeke screwed up her courage and drove into Albuquerque to meet with the setup team for that night's tactical plan. After the formal introductions, the team leader passed out assignments and Zeke went downstairs where a couple of staffers waited to transform her into eye candy.

They put together a top-of-the-line outfit complete with jewelry. They guessed right and the black sheath with a revealingly low cut neckline fit her perfectly. It would be appropriate for the girlfriend of a junior drug lord—sexy with a little bit of class.

Zeke tried, but there was no way to wear a bra so she just had to deal with feeling exposed. The brightly colored Donna Karan sequined jacket extended below her hips and actually felt comfortable. She worried that it might be too tight across her shoulders, but it was all right.

One of the setup team laid out various makeup items. "I have to tell you, Agent Cabot, that combination of a colored jacket and black dress really accentuates your skin tones and makes your gold-tinged brown eyes really pop. Very hot."

"Thank you." Zeke sat still as the woman sponged makeup beneath her eyes. She sat mesmerized by the transformation they were making. There were only a dozen times in her life that Zeke could remember fussing with hair or makeup—other than disguises. Her stint in Washington required her to attend more than one high profile event as part of her job. On those rare occasions, she was aware that her height and physique attracted a lot of attention. On one such assignment, her happily married male partner even hit on her. The office gang never let him forget it.

When the team finished fussing with her hair and makeup, they added gold jewelry including necklaces, bracelets, and earrings. The final touch was a pair of Louboutin's peep toe black heels.

Zeke worried that she looked too much like a tricked-out prostitute, and the four inch heels made her over six feet tall. Just walking and those shoes became an Olympic challenge.

She returned to the conference room, which fell silent as she entered, followed quickly by catcalls and whistles. Zeke still blushed even though she played parts like this before and knew it was all part of the job.

Carlos Griego would be her partner that night. He arrived decked out in a fancy black suit with a very fine pin stripe, black silk shirt and a yellow tie. He had his share of gold jewelry, slicked back hair, and a pair of expensive sunglasses. Built like a running back, at six foot five, he normally towered over everyone, but tonight he was only an inch are so taller than Zeke.

They talked briefly about the game plan. Zeke's new identity was Delta Rae, a well-financed high roller from New Orleans. The team would work as back-up with prearranged code words and signals. Since the meeting would occur at a downtown hotel, Zeke and Carlos would go in without weapons. Other agents positioned as hotel staff and another team posted outside would back them up.

The cocktail/birthday party celebrated a new business venture, which would be opening in the South Valley. Zeke and Carlos were to connect with as many individuals as possible and identify any known felons or gang affiliations. Zeke had a prototype of a high-tech cell phone with a powerful camera that she could use without detection.

This type of undercover operation was nothing new for Zeke or for Carlos. Their limo arrived on time and deposited the couple at the front door of the hotel. The agent driving remained nearby. A waiter directed them to one of the ballrooms where they mingled with nearly a hundred other nattily dressed partygoers. A local band provided pulsing beat that made conversation difficult and recording almost impossible.

"Shit, this could take all night." Carlos grumbled. He immediately donned his best smarmy smile.

They proceeded to the bar where they each ordered a cocktail to carry around for the evening.

Zeke made a good show of hanging on Carlos' arm while whispering in his ear. His support made her less fearful of falling and making an ass of herself. Zeke looked around and thought they made a handsome couple compared to a mostly younger crowd who looked more like a pack of hungry young wolves. The men prowled the room with a feral kind of tension and their conversation sounded more like sparring. Zeke recognized the attitude and thought this event might be more like some kind of gang competition. The air crackled with tension and testosterone.

Carlos did most of the talking and handed out some impressive looking business cards listing him as a real estate broker. As he collected cards and information from dozens of people, Zeke memorized details, descriptions, and body language. One of her gifts had always been a keen eye for detail and her ability to judge people and remember faces. Whenever possible, she affected a bored posture and began using her phone as though she were texting. She was able to take dozens of wide-angle photographs for lab analysis.

Two hours into their job, Carlos put his arm around Zeke and escorted her to a small settee near the restrooms. While appearing very affectionate, Carlos identified a handful of very important suspects and asked her to try to make contact. He explained those individuals appeared to be highly suspicious and unusually well guarded. If she could earn their confidence, she might be able to introduce Carlos.

As he disappeared into the men's room, Zeke moved casually to the bar and positioned herself within the sight line of her first target. He was a fortyish Mexican businessman that she recognized as someone who might have a connection to the Sinaloa drug cartel in Mexico. He held court all evening while anchored at the end of the bar. Zeke watched him for almost twenty minutes. On three or four occasions, she caught his eye, but he made no move.

She was about to give up, when a younger Hispanic male approached her and told her that Señor Santiago would like to buy her a drink. She nodded and he escorted her to the end of the bar.

She knew Carlos watched from a distance, as did the three other alert agents moving unseen throughout the crowd as service personnel.

"My compliments, Señorita." He took her hand and kissed it lightly. "Thank you for joining me. I must tell you how difficult it is for a man to talk business when such a beautiful woman is nearby."

"Why thank you, sir, for your kind words." Zeke displayed her finest smile and syrupy drawl.

The social dance of small talk began. Both smiled graciously and lied—and they both knew it. Señor Santiago, dressed in a very expensive Armani suit, had a rapier wit and a charming manner. Zeke suspected it

126

was a cover for a very shrewd businessman. As they stood, Zeke guessed he was close to six feet tall and solidly built. His shiny black hair waved back behind his ears and on his large hands were two very distinctive gold rings. One had a large emerald cut diamond in a heavy setting and the other had a serpentine design with rubies set for the eyes.

After some superficial small talk, he got around to asking about her escort, whom she carefully described as a very close 'business' associate. He smiled. "Charming, perhaps I might become one of your business associates."

Zeke only smiled wider. "Perhaps you might, but for now, I must rejoin my date. Thank you so much for the drink and the conversation." She extended her right hand, which he kissed gallantly then handed her a business card.

"I will be in town until Wednesday. Perhaps you might join me for lunch?"

"It is certainly a possibility, good night." Zeke held his gaze for a brief moment then turned slowly and walked away feeling his eyes on her. Relief washed over her. She was certain that he had bought her act and was interested. This man could be a valuable asset, but a dangerous one.

Carlos motioned her over to a small group, introducing her to the three men. They had all seen her talking to Señor Santiago. Hell, everyone in the ballroom had seen her talking to him. This might well be the most important contact they had made all evening. Unfortunately, it would fall on Zeke to play this contact should the need arise.

By nine thirty p.m., Zeke and Carlos made their exit. Both were exhausted and relieved to leave the ballroom. Although the goal was always to make it look easy, Zeke was painfully aware of how much effort this kind of undercover role demanded. The minute they arrived in the ballroom, Zeke had been on high alert and adrenalin flooded her system for over two hours. Her limbs felt jittery as though she had been mainlining caffeine.

In the limo, the team exchanged stories while Zeke remained silent and held it together. By the time they reached the office, all of them were ready to call it a night. Zeke grabbed her things and made a beeline for the parking lot. As soon as she got in the car, she began to tremble. Whether from fatigue or fear, she was glad to be in the safety of her vehicle. *I made it without a meltdown and I at least put my toe in the water.*

When she finally arrived home, it was close to eleven and the light was on in the bedroom. When Zeke walked in, Anne dropped the book she was reading, looked up at her, and gasped.

"Oh my, God! Who are you and what've you done with Zeke?"

Zeke smiled as she kicked off the high heels and sat down on the side of the bed. "I don't know how women do this every day."

"Zeke, honestly you look breathtakingly beautiful. You should've been a model. Stand up and turn around. That is a great outfit. Can you keep it?"

"No. I'll take it all back tomorrow morning. I was just too tired tonight." She removed the jewelry and hung up the very expensive outfit then gratefully got into the shower to purge herself of the makeup and the pounds of hair product. After brushing her teeth, she crawled into bed next to Anne and curled up behind her. "I'm so glad to be home."

Chapter Twelve

Zeke stumbled downstairs the next morning where Anne was industriously cleaning out cupboards. Anne poured her some coffee and received a morning kiss.

"I do like this Zeke better." Anne snuggled close for several more warm kisses. "Don't you think it's fun to dress up once in awhile?"

"I haven't done it for a real occasion in so many years that I don't know. It's usually meant that I'd be undercover, which wasn't necessarily fun. When I was in Washington, my girlfriend and I used to dress up occasionally to go to the symphony or to a gallery opening. I guess I enjoyed it."

"You've never mentioned her," Anne said. *A girlfriend? How many more secrets?*

"There isn't much to tell. We were together for a couple of years, but it was kind of a superficial relationship. There was a physical attraction, but nothing very deep. Mostly I guess it was a social convenience. It suited both of our needs."

Anne cocked her head to one side and nodded. "Were you in love with her?"

Zeke looked into her eyes. "No, Annie, I wasn't in love with her. We enjoyed a companionable relationship. More like ships passing in the night because we were both so busy." Zeke refilled her coffee cup. "What're you up to today?"

Okay, end of discussion. "Oh, I've got some chores to do and I told Andrew he could come over to pick up his books in a little while. He was supposed to come last weekend, but I was out of town. What about you?"

"I have to return these fancy duds," she held up the clothing bag on her arm, "so that I'm not charged for them. Then I thought we might be able to take a walk or something."

"Sounds perfect. I'll see you a little later then?"

"Sooner than later, I hope." Zeke embraced Anne and kissed her warmly then walked out the back door.

†

Once in her car, Zeke merged onto the highway and activated her Bluetooth . She hadn't called T.J. for over a week and knew her friend would be worried about her.

"Is this really Zeke Cabot calling?"

Zeke laughed. "It is I, delinquent friend, and desert nomad. How are you Teej?"

"Getting ready to put out an APB for my lost home girl."

"I'm sorry. What with leaving Chicago, meeting up with another agent in Flagstaff, and trying to lure the love of my life over there for the weekend, I lost track of time. When Annie and I made it back to Albuquerque we had a ton of stuff to do for me to get settled in and her to return to work."

"I'm just glad you called. How've you been feeling?"

Zeke paused trying to decide how much she wanted to share with her oldest friend. "I'm set up with the new psychiatrist who seems pretty good. And my transfer was approved so it looks like I'll be back on the clock in less than a month."

"I hope it turns out to be what you expect. Cheryl and I are going to miss you. I finally got used to having you around and there you go again—it just seems sort of sudden."

Zeke felt a lump form in her throat hearing her friend pause. T.J. had always been there for her and it seemed she never got the chance to pay her back. She wasn't around when T.J. and Cheryl moved into their new house. She was in Europe when T.J. had knee surgery. Small wonder she had so few friends. If anyone asked, Zeke would have vehemently denied being unreliable. But she still felt crappy. "I'm sure it does, T.J., but I would've been transferred by the end of the year anyway. This way, I made the choice. I think it's important to give this new relationship a chance. Anne has been so supportive and I need that right now."

"I know, I understand. I sure hope we won't lose touch once you get all cozy."

"No matter what, you will always be my oldest and dearest friend. No matter where I am or who I'm with, you will always be 'numero uno'. I mean it, T.J.. Nothing can change that. Hey, maybe we could arrange something for you guys to come visit."

"I'll talk to Cheryl and see what she has planned for us and let you know. Take care of yourself, Z. We'll talk soon."

Zeke hung up. The lump in her throat had moved down to the pit of her stomach. She heard the disappointment in T.J.'s voice. *I've gotta stop doing this to her and be a better friend.*

When Zeke arrived at the office to return the jewelry and wardrobe, several of the employees greeted her with smiles. This could only mean that the gossip mill was already working and the operation must have been reasonably successful. She continued downstairs with a little more bounce in her step. After the dreadful events of her Chicago case, it felt good to have a little success. One of the agents, who had worked as a hotel employee for the evening, stopped her and told her that the pictures produced some solid leads and evidence. After chatting for a couple of minutes, he thanked her. Zeke quickly made an exit before someone asked her to do something.

✝

Forty-five minutes after Zeke left for the office, Andrew arrived at the back door where Anne greeted him. "Come in, Andrew. I was just cleaning out some cupboards. Do you want some coffee?" She hadn't seen him since the acrimonious divorce and they only talked twice on the phone. An unbelievable mix of feelings flooded her senses—anger, sadness, betrayal, and wariness.

He went past her to the doorway of the family room and looked around. His blond curly hair was longer but thinner on top. He'd also put on some weight and lost the boyish look he had that always made him so attractive. He looked weary and haggard.

"No, thanks. Looks like you've been making some changes. I can't say that I like them, but then you always had strange ideas about decorating." His laugh was shallow.

Anne swallowed the bile in her throat and gritted her teeth as she shoved the box of books closer to the back door. *He'll only be here for a minute.* She returned to her task, pulled a stack of pots and pans out of a lower cupboard, and banged them on the counter.

Andrew sauntered over to the kitchen island and leaned over it. "Do you remember Paul, the junior partner in my firm?"

"I think so, why?" Anne refilled her bucket of

soapy water.

"He said he saw you a few weeks ago at the Prairie Star Restaurant. Do you remember seeing him?"

Anne paused. She fondly remembered having a very romantic dinner at the Prairie Star—their first date. She didn't remember seeing anyone but Zeke. "No, I didn't see him."

"He remembers seeing you. You were having dinner with a woman, an attractive rather handsome looking woman, according to Paul."

"And that's somehow your business?"

"It is when it affects 'my' professional reputation," he snarled. "What do you think people are saying about my ex-wife and a 'girl' friend? It's embarrassing."

Anne turned around and was surprised to find him standing directly behind her. "What I do in public or in private is none of your damn business. And as for your professional reputation, you single-handedly destroyed 'that' all by yourself four years ago."

"You are such a selfish bitch. You always have to make it about you, don't you? You never supported me, and now you're telling me that some dyke girlfriend is better than I was!"

"Oh, yes, Andrew. She's better, so much better. And you know what else? She's honest, caring, and gentle. Oh, and she's an incredible 'lover'."

Anne saw Zeke appear at the door and didn't see the blow that struck her face. Her watering eyes blinked as she suddenly spotted Zeke lunge and execute a perfectly placed kick between his legs that was forceful enough to expel the air from his lungs.

He crumbled to the floor in a heap. When he finally opened his eyes, he saw the barrel of an automatic gun three inches from his forehead.

"FBI, don't move. Annie, are you okay?"

Anne nodded. "Andrew, I'd like you to meet Zeke Cabot, my 'lover'. Zeke, this is Andrew, my stupid, self absorbed, asshole ex-husband."

Anne watched as Zeke's face contorted with rage, but when she spoke, it was quiet and ominous. "If you ever come near this woman again, 'you' will regret it. Do I make myself clear?"

Andrew staggered to his feet, breathing heavily as he cradled his swelling scrotum, "I could sue you, you fucking bitch."

"Just give me a reason." Zeke shoved the gun hard into his cheek.

He turned on his heel and fled through the door.

Zeke stood at the front door to be sure he was gone. Anne waited in the family room watching. She curled up in the corner of the couch and began to cry. "Dammit, he can still make me so mad."

"I know he does." Zeke joined Anne on the couch and pulled her close.

After a few minutes, Anne settled and described their conversation. "I never knew he could be so hateful and ugly."

They remained curled together until Anne relaxed.

Zeke finally said, "Why don't you let me help you with those cupboards?"

"Okay. I'm sure glad you got home when you did." She laughed. "The look on his face was priceless. You sure surprised him."

"I thought I showed considerable restraint."

"I think you did too." Anne began to giggle. "I'd love to be a fly and the wall when he tries to explain why he's not 'in the mood' to his girlfriend." As they worked side by side, Anne seemed less tense. "Can I tell you something weird?"

"By all means." Zeke closed the cupboard door and

leaned back.

"I had the most peculiar sensation when you were confronting Andrew. I was scared when he hit me, then when you were threatening him, I—well, I was kind of turned on. Does that sound crazy?" A blush covered her cheeks.

"Actually—no, not really. I felt the same way but thought it was rude to make a move on you when you were crying your eyes out. I've had that same sensation in the past after a dangerous situation ends. I think it has to do with adrenaline and hormones, you know—arousal. I've heard the guys talk about it a lot. How sex was so much better after a big operation."

They both stopped the busy work.

"Really?" Anne cocked her head as the clinical implications of brain chemistry swirled through her head. "That does make sense. I mean adrenaline amps up everything, so why not lust. Have you ever done anything kind of kinky or unusual?" Anne asked.

Zeke barked a small nervous laugh. "Oh, God, what next? Are you going to tell me that you're into S&M, bondage or fetishes?"

Anne stopped suddenly and blushed. "Well, I don't think so. It's not something I've studied. I guess I've been a bit sheltered."

"And perhaps you think that all lesbians indulge in wild orgiastic sex?"

"Now you're making fun of me."

"No I'm not, hon. I was just teasing you. I'm sorry." Zeke took her face and kissed her very softly. "I'm game, if you're curious." She nibbled at Anne's earlobe. "We're both adults, we can play a little and experiment, it might be fun."

Anne's eyes lit up and she wrapped her arms around Zeke's waist gripping her firmly. "Like what could we do?"

"There are body paints, sex toys, of all varieties or scented oils, that you can buy and…I do have a pair of handcuffs, but…" Zeke kissed Anne's forehead.

Anne returned the kiss. "Let's do that."

"Do what?"

"I want you to handcuff me to the bed." Anne ran her tongue over Zeke's lips hoping to persuade her.

"Are you serious?"

"Well, if you'd prefer, I'll handcuff you." Anne smiled and playfully bit Zeke's lower lip.

Zeke cringed. "Um—as much as I trust you, I'm a little uncomfortable with the idea of being restrained."

"I understand." Anne kissed the base of her throat. "It might be easier for you to be in control, and I might like that better myself. I trust you, Zeke. I need you to understand that." She pulled Zeke toward the stairs teasingly while slowly stripping off her clothes.

†

When they got to the bedroom, Zeke carefully removed each piece of Anne's clothing sending electric sparks shooting up Anne's spine. Her naked and vulnerable body radiated heat and longing.

They stood very close, both breathing hard and filled with desire. Zeke trailed one finger down the gold chain to the glittering Pegasus lying between Anne's sensitive breasts, which reacted instantly to her touch.

"Zeke I'm really turned on right now."

"I know, I am too. You look amazing and your eyes are filled with fire."

"That's not what's on fire."

Anne reached for her, but Zeke grinned and took Anne by the arms. "Just sit here for a minute and don't speak. I'm not sure I can do this—My God, I want you so badly but I don't want hurt you."

"You are so precious to me." Anne stroked Zeke's face. "I want you to make love to me, the way only you can. I want to feel only your touch—please do this."

"Okay, but no handcuffs," Zeke said. "Do you have any scarves? I can do that."

"In the top drawer."

Zeke blindfolded her and moved her to the bed. "I want you to be absolutely sure. Are you still okay with this?"

"Oh, yes, it feels kind of naughty." Anne lay still as Zeke tied one scarf to her right arm, pulled it up to the head of the bed. She started to speak.

"No talking, just relax." A scarf filled her mouth.

Anne felt disoriented, excited, and a little nervous as Zeke pulled her left arm up and attached the scarf. She shook her head and struggled, trying to make a sound. She cried out again.

Zeke pulled the scarf from her mouth and pushed the other one off her eyes. "What's wrong? Are you okay?"

"I couldn't breathe and felt like I was suffocating."

"Okay, we can stop."

"No, I don't want to stop. I just don't want to be gagged."

"Is the blindfold okay?"

"Yes, that's okay."

Zeke reapplied it and touched Anne's cheek. "You can say stop anytime you want."

Anne lay on her back with both hands stretched over her head. She felt the soft silk scarf loop around her ankle and pulled as far as it would go to the side of the bed and then tied the other leg. It felt like she was one of those delicate butterflies stretched and pinned to a black velvet board. Her nakedness and vulnerability made her senses come alive. Every smell, sound, sensation, and touch invaded her heightened awareness with pleasure. The blower on the furnace and a branch scraping on the window with the wind were the only sounds. Sometimes she felt a breath of air waft across the fine hairs on her naked body. She strained to locate Zeke's presence in the room, but couldn't. Then, she heard water running in the bathroom and smelled the green tea soap.

The scarf had dried her mouth; the running water made her a little thirsty. The scarves tightened when she tried to move her arms. The discomfort only amplified her physical need and the immobility focused all her attention to the nerves and muscles between her legs, which ached with wanting, begging for release. Anne's body thrummed with energy from the minute Zeke had agreed to 'play' and now the waiting was unbearable. She shifted her hips restlessly. Unable to see, her senses scanned for any nuance. Her arms bound above her head prickled, she wrapped her fingers around the cold wrought iron of the headboard. Although the bedding was warm, she had goose bumps of anticipation. They hadn't talked about what was going to happen and it was clear that Zeke wouldn't offer anything further.

There was another sound in the room, the hiss of the gas fireplace as Zeke ignited it. Anne heard movement and felt the mattress give as Zeke moved onto the bed next to her. At first, there was nothing but the sound of breathing, slow and regular and then Anne felt first one, then two warm fingers trailing across her abdomen and breasts then down her outer thigh. The muscles beneath her skin sent tiny electric shocks to her spine. The touching and light stroking continued for long savory moments exciting her skin and her mind as she pictured Zeke's long fingers brushing along her body caressing her arms, neck, and chest. The embers of desire flashed causing a twitchy discomfort. She sucked air through her mouth.

Anne surrendered to the firestorm of physical sensations and allowed her body to writhe with yearning, unable to satisfy her craving. The touching stopped as hot lips grazed then enveloped her breast. She gasped and jolt shot down her spine arching her back and causing the small muscles to tighten. A flick of Zeke's tongue preceded the sucking sensation, sending ripples of pleasure through her body. Anne bit her lip to muffle a groan from deep in her belly. Her thoughts dissolved as her breathing sped up. She pulled at the restraints in vain. A coppery taste in her mouth was from biting her lip to keep from screaming.

It seemed like an eternity of throbbing anticipation until those delicate strong fingers found their way to the desperately swollen tissues between her straining legs. The unseen fingers carefully stroked all of the surrounding skin above and below and on either side. After several minutes of repetitive stroking meant to both relax and excite, Anne felt one finger moving toward her wet, throbbing center. She froze, trying to command her traitorous body to wait a little longer.

Zeke added another finger, moving deeper and more rhythmically.

The intensity grew unbearably through each fiber of her trembling body. Anne shook. When the tidal spasms began, Anne dug her heels into the mattress and rode the waves of pleasure, locking Zeke's hand in place. Perspiration covered her heaving chest as every muscle surrendered. "Yessss."

"I love you." Zeke slid the blindfold off and untied

the scarves.

The trembling subsided, as Anne lay spent, unable to talk, aware that Zeke had moved away from the bed and then to the bathroom. Gentle waves of pleasure washed gently over her damp skin. "Amazing. Oh, Zeke. Oh my, God. I don't know what to say." The warm air felt good as she filled her lungs then exhaled and rolled onto her side. "That's a totally different sensory experience. It's hard to describe but the restraints seemed to amplify every sensation and there were no distractions. God, I'm still tingling. Baby, was it weird for you?"

Anne watched as Zeke put things away, then stretched out next to Anne, and kissed her palm. After a pause she said, "It was a little scary at first, seeing you so vulnerable and trusting. But, I guess I can see what you mean. Being an anonymous lover felt sort of freeing. I love you" She stroked Anne's cheek and smiled.

Anne put her finger on Zeke's lips and searched her face wanting to reconnect. "Honestly, that just blew my mind. Your hands—your lips, I felt so completely yours." Anne kissed Zeke softly.

"Making love to you gives me so much pleasure, because I can show you how much you mean to me and it gets better every single time. And trusting me—you have no idea how much it helps." Zeke pulled her very close and pressed her lips the hard against Anne's temple.

†

Sunday morning began with leisurely coffee drinking and lounging on the sofa with the sunshine pouring over the Sunday paper.

"I like this." Anne brushed her finger through the hair around Zeke's ear.

"My ear?"

"Well, yes, your ears are quite lovely. I meant lazy Sunday mornings curled up with the most amazing woman I've ever met."

Zeke took her hand and kissed each fingertip.

Anne giggled and felt her cheeks flush. "I know this is going to sound silly, but I just never get tired of looking at you. You have the most beautiful features and gorgeous skin. But your mouth is, my God, delicious, sensuous, and quite versatile." As if to make a point, she outlined Zeke's lips with her finger.

Zeke tossed her newspaper aside and pulled Anne into her lap. "Thank you."

"Looking into your eyes I feel drawn in and breathless. Please kiss me." Time seemed to stand still. Those beautiful features, only inches from her face held her speechless and immobile. It was hard to breathe and she wanted nothing more than to etch this moment in her memory forever.

Zeke moved her hand to caress Anne's cheek and licked her lower lip.

Zeke's eyes were unblinking as Anne reached around and held the back of Zeke's neck. Their breathing synchronized and Anne closed her eyes as her lips felt the lightest touch of breath.

The back of Zeke's fingers brushed her cheek and soft lips hovered gently over her mouth. Her heart raced and small muscles in her belly began to tighten. An eternity passed before the feather light touches changed from a prelude to an irresistible invitation.

Anne surrendered to the intermittent touches and withdrawals, each one pulling her deeper until neither could resist the intimate connection. There were soft sounds as each shared in the dance. Their lips and tongues provided lyrics. "I never realized that a kiss could be a life altering experience," Anne said.

Zeke pulled back, caressing her face, smiled, and suddenly began to chuckle. "Just a part of my all inclusive service."

"Really, do any of your other services include barn work?"

"What did you have in mind?" Zeke began nuzzling Anne's ear.

Anne reluctantly disengaged and stood up. "Stop. I need to take care of the horses and thought you might like to help."

"I would be happy to help you with anything."

†

Dressed in jeans, jackets, and work boots, they walked the short distance to the stable to begin Zeke's training in Horsemanship 101. Although it was nearly noon, a northwesterly breeze from the crest chilled the air. Once they got busy working, it wouldn't matter as much.

While Zeke grew up in the south, she considered herself an urban girl. She respected and appreciated most animals but avoided them. Of course, there was also that snake issue.

Anne reintroduced her to Shadow, the agreeable horse who had carried them off the mountain after Zeke injured her ankle several weeks prior.

Zeke gingerly patted his neck. "I don't know if I properly thanked you for rescuing me from that treacherous hiking trail."

Anne laughed. "I'm not sure the trail was so treacherous. Maybe it was Zeke the inexperienced hiker."

"That is not fair. My life was threatened." Zeke squawked.

Anne handed her a currycomb then quickly demonstrated how to brush the horse before she moved to the next stall to groom Sunny, the smaller brown and white Paint.

Zeke stayed with Shadow and carefully brushed him the way Anne showed her. The stable quickly warmed with their activity and the heat emanating from the large horses. She inhaled the rich, earthy smells from the animals and the straw. A couple of birds flittered about the ceiling trusses making the only other sound other than the soft nickers or occasional snorts from the horses.

As they mucked out the stalls, Zeke marveled at the way Anne moved the huge animals aside with no apparent concern for injury. They worked for a couple of hours cleaning the barn, sweeping the floors, making sure there was hay and grain ready and the water tank rinsed out.

Anne finally put away the pitchforks while Zeke rinsed the empty wheelbarrow. They sat on a large hay bale and watched as the two horses wandered the corral. It was hard work, but it felt good to be physically tired instead of mentally exhausted.

"Zeke, I think we got sidetracked when we were talking about Dr. Taylor yesterday. What else did she say?" Anne leaned back against the tack room wall and stroked Zeke's back.

"We talked about different things, you know, she's nothing like Dr. Nilsson, she's much younger and more direct. She doesn't beat around the bush." Zeke wasn't sure how to tell Anne what she needed to say. "I guess she doesn't need to waste time because she has my records from Chicago. I appreciated the fact that we didn't have to start from square one. She even gave me some homework, which I haven't done."

"Yeah, you said that, but the homework, what did she want you to do? Can I help?"

"She wanted me to explore my emotional response to the assault and to share those feelings with you. You and I didn't really discuss everything because I, well—I couldn't. I really appreciate the fact that you gave me the space and didn't press the matter. Then I left town quickly, so it really hasn't come up again."

Anne pulled on Zeke's arm and she scooted back against the wall until they were side-by-side holding hands. "I think she's right, hon. We can't ignore the elephant in the room forever, and I do care about how you felt and how you feel now."

Zeke took a deep breath as though she were diving into deep water. "Okay. I guess I can try." Her chest tightened along with the muscles in her throat. With great effort and in a voice choked with pain Zeke cleared her throat before she began to speak. "I didn't want to think about it ever again, but I guess the whole awful event has been processing in my brain somewhere. When I started to retell Dr. Nilsson how scared and angry I was, I realized that I failed and blamed myself for what happened and for not being alert and prepared. I was scared that you'd be hurt if I did anything foolish. A small part of me also blames you and our relationship for distracting me."

There was a deafening silence.

Anne pulled her hand away, stood slowly then walked over to the fence and gripped the top rail as hard as she could. She was trembling with anger, pain, and sadness. She was breathing hard and tears stung her eyes. Was it her imagination, or did the love of her life just blame her for being assaulted?

Zeke came up behind her and put a hand on her shoulder.

Anne whirled around. "Don't touch me," her eyes narrowed, "how dare you blame me for what happened! I have done everything to care for you, protect you, and support you, including sending you back to Chicago! What the fuck do you mean by blaming me?"

Zeke grabbed her by both arms and lowered her voice. "Please, Annie, let me explain."

Anne pulled against the firm grip desperately. "No! I don't want to hear anymore."

"I'm not finished, and I need you to listen." The grip tightened. "I can't do this without you. I need you, and I love you. I 'know' in my head that you were not to blame. I understand that now. God, I'm making a mess of this, but I'm trying to explain to you why it screwed me up so badly."

Anne, trembling with rage, wrenched herself free from Zeke's hold and backed into the fence.

Zeke shoved her hands in her jacket pockets.

Anne remained firm, pushing back against the fence.

Zeke took a deep breath. "Please just listen a minute, Annie. Our trip to Taos was, and will always be, magical for me, especially our first night together. I've never been happier in my life. I was still high the whole day Saturday, feeling drunk with passion and utter bliss. It felt so good words can't do it justice. What I didn't mention early, because I didn't think it was important, was that I had received some warnings about internet 'chatter' about me earlier in the week. Agent Donovan and I had talked on a couple of occasions."

"Why couldn't you have just said something?" Anne hated the pain she saw in Zeke's face.

Zeke shook her head. "All day Saturday I had a sense that something was off or that we were being followed but I never spotted anyone. I deliberately picked that place we stopped for lunch because it provided a better view of the road. Since I never saw anything by the time we reached Columbine Creek, I had completely let my guard down. We started kissing, my libido kicked into high gear and I started dreaming about another night like our first. When they knocked on the window, I couldn't react fast enough.

"Once I finally put two coherent thoughts together, my first was for your safety then how to get you out of there." Zeke's words came faster as she wrapped her arms around her waist. "I wasn't sure what you might do, and I didn't want you hurt. I was so scared, but I couldn't use my weapon because I had stupidly left it under the seat. They had control—with a gun shoved against your head." Gulping air, she squeezed her eyes tight.

Anne could do nothing but encourage her to continue.

"The other guy was rubbing against me. Shit, I was scared and angry. God, dammit, I'm a professional and I should never have let that happen." Her jaw clenched. "When the guy started threatening you to force me to talk...I...I didn't know what to do. All I could think was that they were going to kill us both and leave us out there." Zeke swallowed hard. "I blamed you. My distorted thinking was that if you hadn't been there, if we hadn't been kissing, if I hadn't fallen in love with you, none of it would've happened. Hell, if it had been a training exercise, they would've thrown me out of the academy. That made me angry, and I needed someone to blame." Zeke's tears began to fall.

They both leaned back against the fence in silence.

Anne's own memory of the pain and suffering they had endured on that fateful day rushed back to her consciousness. She deflated. Her anger evaporated as she tried to imagine herself in Zeke's place. Would she have felt the same way?

Zeke coughed and cleared her throat. "After talking to Dr. Taylor, though, I figured out that the consuming self-loathing I felt was that I had not done my job to protect us. I couldn't accept that responsibility because the pain was too much. In my mind, I guess I needed a scapegoat." Zeke put her hand on Anne's sleeve very softly. "Annie, don't you see, I felt it was my fault that I had not taken control of the situation at the outset. That situation should not have happened." She dropped her arm to her side. "Once I came to grip with that and realized that my emotional self was in the driver's seat that day, I felt worthless and ashamed."

Zeke turned to Anne and leaned her arms heavily on the fence. "Dr. Taylor wanted me to be honest with you because our relationship can't grow if we can't share that kind of honesty. But, I'm just no good at talking about this shit. I hate that I hurt you by blurting it out so thoughtlessly, because I would never do anything to harm you. Annie, I would've given up my life to keep you safe that day. Do you understand?"

Anne could only stare into those brown eyes. She felt angry, scared, hurt, and sad. The past few weeks had been both heaven and hell for both of them. "Zeke, I hear what you're saying, and I understand, but I can't help feeling hurt." Anne turned and walked back to the house in silence.

Chapter Thirteen

The brisk early morning temperatures of November rose quickly as the sun hit the eastern slopes of the Sandia Mountains. Hints of frost glazed the branches on the upper slopes of the mountain. Fewer birds visited the feeders and most days migrating birds flew overhead on their way south.

Both women started the week early on Monday morning.

Anne hurried off to town to pick up supplies before seeing her first patient.

Zeke stood by the garage door bundled up and watched her drive off. Without their usual morning banter, Zeke felt hollow. Instead of mentally rehashing the dreadful confrontation, she chose a brisk walk down the driveway through the sparsely populated neighborhood to try to focus on something distracting. The gravel road covered with multicolored leaves muffled her footsteps.

Most of the lots were probably five or ten acres with the homes set back off the communal road and surrounded by shrubbery. It felt more like a walk in the woods. The homes were large and more traditional in appearance, unlike the majority of homes in New Mexico which were adobe and southwestern in design. Zeke imagined that many of the residents were transfers from out of state, perhaps easterners.

The air smelled fresh and crisp with just a hint of piñon smoke. It felt good to stretch her legs and get her blood moving. Heaviness weighed on her from the discussion with Anne. They hadn't really spoken much after that. There was polite conversation about daily activities including meals. Anne had kissed her good night, but slept restlessly. Zeke blamed herself and Dr. Taylor.

There were good reasons to compartmentalize things, and this misunderstanding was a perfect example. Sometimes honesty hurt people. And this time it hurt someone she loved. Zeke kicked the small branch lying in front of her and watched as it bounced helplessly a few feet down the road—she knew how it felt to be bouncing helplessly. She sighed deeply. Until Anne felt like talking, she could do nothing to make the situation better. On impulse, she pulled out her cell phone and punched in T.J.'s number.

"Hi, Zeke. What a nice surprise."

"Hey, T.J., You know me, feast, or famine. Have you got a minute?"

"Sure, what's up?"

"I think I messed up. The new therapist suggested I talk to Anne about how I felt after the assault. Well the truth is that for a while I blamed Anne for distracting me to the point of being unprepared."

"Tell me you didn't say that."

"Yeah, that's exactly what I did."

"Dear God, Zeke, what were you thinking? Did she throw you out of the house? I sure would have."

"No, but we're really not talking. It's my fault. I know there's a better way to talk about these things, but I'm just not used to it. I don't talk about feelings, and that's why—it just opens a nasty can of worms."

There was a long pause. "You have got to figure out a way to make this right. Girl, you weren't kidding when you said you messed up."

An aching sadness grew in Zeke's chest when she

thought of losing Anne. "I know. I just don't know what to do."

"Don't beat yourself up anymore. The damage is done. Can you think of something to let her know how much you care? I know she's really important to you and you can't let this get in the way."

"Do you think I should ask her to go to the therapist with me?"

"I don't know. That might not be such a great idea. It might be better to let this die down a little bit. Maybe you could get her some flowers or a nice card or something."

"Thanks, I will. I'll let you go now. Take care."

She put the phone back in her pocket as her eyes burned from the tears. *How could I have been so stupid? The most unbelievable woman I've ever met and I go and screw it up. Dammit.*

When she reached the end of the road, she continued up through the woods as her mind searched frantically for the words—any words—that might make sense to absolve her. There was none. She was getting nowhere letting the guilt bounce around inside her skull like a ping-pong ball. *Work. Do something.*

†

Energized by the exercise, Zeke returned to the house, made fresh coffee, and threw herself into her case notes. Whenever the emotional heat became unbearable, work had been her refuge. She glanced at the calendar sitting on her desk—the beautiful desk Anne arranged for her—as she booted her computer.

The vacation/medical leave would be over in a couple of weeks. After much thought, she had submitted the formal transfer request for the

Albuquerque field office and approval followed. She leaned her head back and stretched the neck muscles. The few belongings she possessed sat in the guest room of Anne Reynolds' home. Her leased car was still in the impound lot of the Albuquerque FBI Field office. The only vaguely familiar things in her life were the expertise and skills of her job and the woman she'd chosen over everything. *This is it. I'm starting over.*

Pages of notes and telephone transcripts demanded her attention. She started with a list of relevant facts related to the Hussein brothers import business and moved things around until a pattern emerged. After comparing the pattern to the subpoenaed bank records, she found some relevant information.

Zeke shook her head, embarrassed she had missed so many clues. Everyone was obsessed with Doctor Ahmed Hussein and his dramatic and senseless killings while his brother stayed under the radar with very little attention. Hassan Hussein had brokered deals with questionable individuals in Central and South America as well as contacts in the Middle East. *How did we miss this?* She circled his name repeatedly.

His regularly scheduled buying trips gave every appearance of a well-planned money-laundering scheme that involved smuggling either drugs or weapons. It was an enormous amount of money, much more than he would make selling imported rugs. It also explained the connection to the cousin selling rugs in Phoenix. Zeke scribbled a sticky note to get the report filed by the field agent who followed up with Mubarak, the Phoenix rug merchant, after her assault.

She leaned back in the comfortable leather chair and thought about the recent trip back through Phoenix with Anne. She chided herself for not taking the side trip to visit Hussein's cousin who sent the two hired thugs after her. She didn't know whether the Phoenix merchant reported directly to Hassan or was nothing more than a supportive relative. Either way, he might continue looking for her.

Zeke walked to the window and stretched her arms against the top frame. The pine trees lining the driveway swayed with the chilly wind. Ominous gray clouds hovered above the mountain crest. It made her shiver almost like an omen.

She glanced over her shoulder at the memo on the computer screen. If Ahmed Hussein's attorneys were successful, and Guantánamo Bay released him to the States, he'd face criminal charges. Should that happen, there was a good possibility that he would want revenge for his CIA rendition.

The fact that the Hussein brothers worked through a larger network than originally known, caused more worry because she realized that other people might be targets including Anne and possibly Zeke's parents. She shivered at the thought of her parents being involved. That was a frightening thought. She started to pace in the small enclosed area. *Okay, don't let this get out of hand. There are practical steps you can take. Just take a breath and focus.* She clenched and unclenched her fists as she tried to slow her breathing. Her heart continued to race. *Think.* Someone tracked her through her credit cards from Chicago to Biloxi then to Albuquerque before they found her.

Zeke sat on the arm of the wingback chair overlooking the corral in front where Anne's two horses grazed. Her life was more complicated now. She had found someone she loved. In the past, she could have packed her few belongings and disappeared into the night. That wasn't an option. She not only couldn't leave, she didn't want to.

The Hussein family invaded her life like some increasingly virulent vermin—you get rid of one and two more appear. In order get rid of the threat, all the vermin had to be exterminated at once.

A sharp pain burned in her solar plexus. Anger, stress, too little sleep, and too much coffee didn't help. Zeke went back to the computer and looked at the screen. Information was a powerful weapon, and the more she could learn, the better her chances. She typed in a request for a few more documents from the agency files then backed up her report on a flash drive.

†

After showering and changing clothes, Zeke drove into the Albuquerque FBI office with her newly discovered information. She picked up an ID badge at the reception desk and waited for the receptionist to buzz her through the door.

Mike Donovan's office was empty, so she moved the chair and sat down. On the left side of the tidy desk sat a digital picture frame containing pictures of a family. His wife could've been a Dallas cheerleader; the two little girls were towheaded princesses. *Mike Donovan, Mr. All American.* Zeke smiled then grabbed a Post-it note. She stuck one on top of her notes just as Special Agent de la Hoya passed by the office and noticed her. "Hello, Agent Cabot. I'm surprised to see you. Anxious to start work?"

"No, ma'am. Actually, I promised to give Mike some numbers he wanted."

"Well, I won't keep you. I just wanted you to know that the team was very impressed with your performance the other night. We got some very good intel."

Zeke fidgeted and tried to straighten her jacket. The chance of running into the boss didn't occur to her when she hastily dressed. "I'm glad it worked out."

"Since you stopped in, can I ask if you'd be willing to meet Señor Santiago again? I know it's a lot to ask, but he's one of the best leads we've had."

The temperature in the room seemed to rise rapidly and Zeke felt like she was suffocating. She pulled her collar and swallowed. "Uh, I was just leaving agent Donovan a note—I really don't have a lot of time."

Agent de la Hoya shook her head and smiled. "Oh, not today. But if you'd be willing to arrange a time with him another day—you could make a phone call from here in the office."

Crap on a cracker. Just tell her no. "What did you have in mind?" Zeke heard the words but didn't believe she had just spoken them.

"Nothing big. A quick daytime meeting—maybe lunch, or something. That way we might be able to get a tail on him. Your call."

Zeke accepted the unregistered cell phone, and took a deep breath trying to recall her improvised character. The heady accolades she'd received from the team boosted her courage. She dialed the number from memory. "Señor Santiago—may I please speak to him? Tell him Delta Rae is on the phone. He'll know." She waited knowing that he would deliberately make her wait.

"Good afternoon, my beautiful *Señorita*, I'm so pleased that you have called. I hope it is because you wish to dine with me."

"How nice of you to remember. I'm sorry it's taken so long for me to reach you, but Carlos and I had some business in Santa Fe."

"When would be a convenient time for you?" Zeke

wasn't surprised that he didn't want to talk on the phone.

"Today is just crazy, you have no idea how many errands I have to run, but tomorrow afternoon looks much better." She read the note provided by her boss. "I will be in the uptown area and there's a wonderful new Italian place—La Cucina—shall we say around two?"

"I'm afraid it would need to be just a little later," said Santiago.

Exert more control, naturally. "I think I could do three," drawled Zeke. "See ya'll then?"

"Perhaps you could give me your telephone number so I could reach you, in case I am detained."

Zeke expected this and provided the number on the disposable cell phone. There would be no way to trace it.

He hung up and Zeke returned to de la Hoya's office to report. They worked out a plan for backup and a setup in the restaurant next door in case he asked for an alternative meeting. That would provide twenty-four hours to plant the surveillance equipment.

Zeke agreed to be at the office by noon to be dressed and made-up.

†

Afraid she would be late for her appointment with Dr. Taylor, Zeke left the building in a hurry. As soon as she got in the car, her cell phone rang, and she smiled at the familiar number on the display, "Hi, Annie, what're you doing?"

"I just finished up with a patient and have one more to see before I stop at the office."

"You sound a little blue, is everything okay?" Zeke

was always concerned when her upbeat lover sounded off and hoped she wasn't still angry.

"Oh, I'm okay. I just needed to hear your voice and to tell you how much I love you. When do you think you'll be home?"

"I'm on my way over to see Dr. Taylor then I should be home right after. Do you need me to pick up anything?"

"No, I'll see you at home."

"Annie, I love you. I'm glad you called."

"Bye, baby."

Zeke put her phone away thinking how much she enjoyed being able to tell someone how much she loved her and feel loved in return. It warmed the cold spot in her chest. She steered the car into the parking lot at two minutes before three.

†

Dr. Taylor spent the first few minutes reviewing Zeke's week and asking about any symptoms or flashbacks she might have had. Zeke surprised herself when she reported that she felt okay and only had a couple of flash backs in the past week.

"Excellent. Were you able to talk with your partner about your emotional reaction and guilt?"

Zeke closed her eyes briefly re-experiencing the painful argument from Sunday followed quickly with a flash of anger. "Well, it didn't go as smoothly as I thought. Yesterday was the first chance I had, and—I'm afraid I didn't present my feelings as clearly as I could have." She glanced up at Dr. Taylor who simply nodded.

"When I said I blamed her, she got really angry and stormed off. It took everything I had to convince her to listen to me. I told her I wasn't inferring that it was 'actually' her fault. I just needed a scapegoat to alleviate my self-hatred. She didn't buy it and we still haven't really talked about that." A sick feeling started in her stomach. "By the time I replayed the conversation again in my head, it became clear to me how much of my self-worth I get from my job. And I realized that I may set my standards a little too high sometimes—for myself and for others." The words were tumbling out faster. "I'm good at my job, but I'm not a perfect human being and it's more than likely that I will screw up again. I can't blame other people for my shortfalls. If I screw up, I have to own it. What I won't do again is ignore that little voice my head that has kept me safe for fifteen years."

"So you no longer think Anne has any responsibility for your inability to respond?"

"No. It was entirely my fault and I should never have blamed her." Zeke could feel the truth of the statement as she said the words.

They refocused on Zeke's career. Dr. Taylor wanted her to think about where she thought her life would be in five years. And then she asked Zeke to look at some new ways of balancing her personal and professional life. They finished by setting another appointment for the following week.

†

Anne was pleased to see her neighbor Susan at the community mailbox as she pulled up.

"Hi there, mystery neighbor. We haven't seen much of you." Susan waved.

"Hi. Susan," Anne shifted the mail to one arm as she gave her neighbor a hug. "You know how I get when the weather turns cold. I turn into a hermit."

"How's it going with your new roommate?"

Anne felt herself blush. "We get along pretty well, I think, but it's only been a couple of weeks. It's nice to have someone to share things with, especially meals."

"I'm glad, Anne. We should have you two over for dinner some night."

"That would be wonderful. I'd like you to meet her."

Susan whooped as she opened a large fancy envelope. "Cool, an invitation to the Santa Fe Gallery party." She frowned. "Darn, that's the one weekend we'll be out of town. I wish I'd known sooner. This is always a wonderful event with lots of interesting people and great food. Wait, maybe you could go?" She offered Anne the invitation.

"Oh, I don't know, I gave up the social scene after the divorce." Anne read the intriguing invitation.

Susan gently put her hand on Anne's arm. "Well, you decide because we can't use it and I think it might be a good opportunity for you to get out and socialize."

Anne drove up to her house thinking about Susan's words and convinced herself it might be fun to hit the Santa Fe social scene and show off the enchanting Zeke Cabot.

"Zeke?" she called as she came in the back door.

No answer.

†

When Zeke arrived home a little after four thirty, Anne greeted her with a warm hug and kiss. "I'm glad you're home. Here let me take that." She hung up Zeke's jacket.

"Thanks, I'm glad to be home. You look happy,

158

what's up?"

Anne stood grinning. "Would you like to accompany me to a glittering evening at the Georgia O'Keefe Gallery in two weeks?"

"I would love to accompany you anywhere on earth."

Anne gave Zeke another big smooch.

Zeke chuckled. "Are you aware of how much time we spend in your kitchen kissing?"

"Of course I am," Anne curled two fingers into Zeke's shirt front, "and it's not nearly enough. I'm afraid we're falling behind. Because it's a proven fact, that you are the best kisser in the universe, your lips the softest and your tongue—why, it should be a licensed weapon." Anne ran her hands around Zeke's waist then up under her shirt.

"Funny you should mention that." Zeke drew her tongue across Anne's lips. "It's registered in thirty different countries." She pulled Anne into her arms as they continued tasting and touching.

"Oh, dear, Lord." Anne groaned softly, as Zeke continued to kiss her face and neck. Anne was quivering as she pulled Zeke even closer and hungrily seized her mouth, thrusting her tongue between her lips. Zeke pressed her hips forward and could feel Anne's knees shake.

"Stop, Zeke, please stop," Anne gasped. "We can't do this now. One of us has to be strong. There's too much to do and you are an incredible temptation."

They disengaged for long enough to attend to some practical matters like feeding the horses and preparing dinner as well as cleaning up their individual work related tasks. Zeke watched Anne with curiosity. She seemed to have let go of yesterday's disagreement.

As they worked side by side, Zeke asked, "How

were your patients today?"

"Actually, the day went quickly. Some routine wound care, and an elderly man that I transferred to hospice care."

"Is that difficult for you? Maybe that's why you were kind of down."

"Yeah, maybe that was it."

Zeke did not press her.

"How about you? What kind of mischief did you get into?"

"Nothing very exciting. I met with Dr. Taylor, and I talked with Agent de la Hoya."

"Oh, you went to the FBI office?"

"I had some papers for Mike and she saw me in his office. She wanted me to help them out again." Zeke focused her attention on her plate to avoid Anne's penetrating glare.

As they talked about Zeke's meeting with Señor 'drug-cartel'—as Anne referred to him—Anne became visibly upset and peppered Zeke with a dozen questions about her safety. Would there be anyone else there? Would she have a microphone? Would she have an escape plan?

Zeke reassured her, and decided that in the future it would be wise to withhold some details about potential operations until 'after' they were completed.

"It's just a quick lunch. They want him to feel more comfortable. It shouldn't take long at all."

By the time they were ready for bed, Zeke thought of her own misgivings about the planned meeting. This time she would be alone with a large and dangerous man. She logically knew nothing much could happen in the restaurant, but her gut clenched with apprehension.

Chapter Fourteen

Zeke arrived at the office on time for the transformation to Miss Delta Rae. She asked the two women assigned to her to find something more casual for her to wear. They returned excitedly with a dozen items to transform the beautiful new agent into the saucy persona of Delta Rae, Carlos' lady.

Zeke viewed the experience with the same enthusiasm she did when the young technician had to wire her—embarrassing and uncomfortable.

When completed, she looked stunning with burgundy colored leather pants that fit like a glove, a low cut cream-colored blouse, and a beautiful cashmere sweater coat of dark purple and blue. Expensive Western boots with three-inch heels and pointed silver tipped toes completed the outfit.

Hair and make-up were high fashion but toned down slightly from the cocktail party. The accessories were sterling silver. An ornate leather satchel containing a wallet with fake ID, credit cards, and a make-up bag completed the ensemble.

As Zeke went through the purse, she marveled at the detail and the quantity of stuff that was in a normal woman's handbag. Even before she joined the Agency, Zeke worked to simplify her style and life. She had little interest or need for material possessions and although she admired and purchased nice things, it was generally necessities.

She pondered the whole effect they created for her, and thought about Anne's reaction to her last dress-up and realized her girlfriend appreciated feminine accoutrements. Anne's gushing approval made her smile.

†

Carlos was reviewing instructions with the small team when Zeke walked in to join them. The room fell silent then the catcalls started. Her temporary popularity was solely due to her appearance. Zeke knew well that actions spoke louder than appearances and it spurred her to do a good job. That was the sole reason she opted to take this assignment. Her official start date was the first of December, so Zeke took this opportunity to make a good impression and become familiar with her coworkers.

There was one other female agent at the table, and Zeke felt her attention the whole time. Zeke recognized some of the others from the Friday night job and nodded as she made eye contact with each of them. When they were ready to head out, Zeke made a point of introducing herself to the other female agent. "I'm Zeke Cabot, the newbie," she extended her hand.

"I'm Molly Bentsen. It's good to meet you finally. I hear you and Carlos scored really good information on Friday."

She sounded sincere, but cautious.

"Well, I hope that pans out, and hopefully I'll get Carlos hooked up today. I don't really enjoy being trussed up like a Christmas goose. It's not my style. I'm more of a denim kind of gal." Zeke smiled warmly. The team leader called her name. "Got to go, see you later."

The boss requisitioned a confiscated cream-colored Cadillac Seville with a warning not to wreck it. Zeke arrived at the uptown shopping center a half hour early.

She wanted the extra time to familiarize herself with the area and the shops.

After passing two or three shops, she entered a small boutique with unique fashions and handcrafted jewelry some of which reminded her of Anne. After looking over several items, she selected a delicate gold bracelet with an intricate pattern and a well-crafted clasp. She paid with the gold Master Card in her wallet and had the receipt with the name Delta Rae on it, because it might add some credence to her background if the card actually had some activity. Plus she had no money with her.

When she arrived at the restaurant purposely late, she found Señor Santiago already seated at a booth in the rear. She sashayed back to the booth apologizing as she neared the table. "I am so sorry. You know I was actually early and I just had to stop at this cute little shop and before you know it, here I am late." Zeke blithered with her drawl and batted her eyes at the slightly confused gentleman.

"It is perfectly all right. I have only just arrived a moment ago." He kissed her hand. "Would you care for a cocktail before lunch?"

"You know, that's an excellent idea. How about one of those delicious margaritas?"

He ordered them each a margarita, an appetizer, and proceeded to regale her with stories of his business successes including the fact that he made monthly trips from his villa in northern Mexico to New Mexico to check on his business. Zeke listened attentively making mental notes of names and dates. She was fully aware that much of what he was telling her was probably bullshit meant to impress her, but that was the purpose of the meeting. She nodded appropriately and sipped her cocktail, offering little information about herself except to say that this was her first trip to New Mexico but that Carlos had told her quite a lot about the area on his frequent visits to see her. She was equally vague about her relationship with him except to say they shared a business interest in his real estate holdings.

They continued the information-volley throughout lunch, and by the end, Señor Santiago expressed an interest in meeting with Carlos the next time he returned to Albuquerque. A real estate investment, which an associate assured him he would appreciate, was his purported interest for the meeting.

He removed a notebook and pen from his pocket, wrote down several phone numbers in Mexico, and instructed her to call when she had spoken to Carlos. She was only to say that this regarded the New Mexico property.

Zeke took the phone numbers, folding the paper and slipping it into her blouse, smiling. As the waiter poured coffee, Señor Santiago moved closer, slid his arm around her, and massaged her shoulder. He continued to whisper in her ear praising her beauty and charm.

His touch burned through her clothes. Zeke began to perspire as her pulse raced. It was not from desire but anxiety. When he pulled her hand into his lap, she felt his erection. Zeke had to fight the panic that was rising up her chest and threatening to suffocate her. She felt lightheaded and short of breath. She wanted to scream and run, but instead, she smiled and moved both of their hands up to the table. "You know, I have had the most delightful lunch, and you are utterly charming but I must go. I am so sorry to eat and run, but I am sure we will meet again." Zeke grabbed her bags and slid out of the booth as quickly as she could, hurrying to the door before her legs betrayed her.

As soon as she was outside, she took a deep breath of fresh air and sagged against the building trembling. Somewhat calmed, she ran to her car. Safely inside, she began to shake uncontrollably. She wrapped her arms around herself and held on for dear life as the flashback from her assault vividly ran through her mind, and she felt the memory of the sweaty, grabbing hands holding her down intent on violating her.

When she finally opened her eyes and managed to slow her breathing, she discovered thirty minutes had passed. "Motherfucker!"

Zeke had to pull it together quickly because the team would be wondering what happened to her. As she drove back to the office by a rather circuitous path, she worked on a story. A quick look in the mirror didn't help. The mascara smeared. She looked pale and frightened. She wiped under her eyes and dug through the purse to see if there was any lipstick.

†

"Hey, look who is back. It's Miss Delta Rae fresh from her show stopping performance at La Cucina." One of the team members stood up from the conference table and applauded.

"We were afraid you had run off to Mexico with him."

They all laughed.

"He sure seems to like his pretty Señorita and I can't say that I blame him!" one of them crooned.

The whole team laughed. No one asked why she took so long to return to the station—Zeke didn't offer.

She presented the highlights of their conversation, including the phone numbers but never offered an explanation about her abrupt departure and quickly made her excuses to leave and change out of her outfit.

Once back in her own clothes, Zeke wrote a check for the bracelet she purchased, put it in an envelope with the receipt, left it on Special Agent de la Hoya's desk, and then hurried out to her car.

As soon as she was alone, the trembling resumed along with hyperventilating. When she got some control, she reached for her phone and tried to dial Dr. Taylor's number three times. She finally reached her voicemail and left a message. "—something happened at work today and I think I should talk to you." She left her call back number and hung up. Even the act of making the phone call helped, so Zeke started the car for her ride home.

As she merged onto Lomas, the phone rang. She glanced at the display and said, "Thank you for calling back so quickly. I'm better now but I had a bit of a meltdown and had to pull out of an undercover detail—yes—on Lomas—okay, I will."

Zeke hung up and turned toward Central where Dr. Taylor would be waiting at her office. She said she didn't like the sound of Zeke's voice.

Dr. Taylor unlatched the door and escorted her into the office, where Zeke collapsed into a chair and tears coursed down her face.

Dr. Taylor handed her tissues and waited.

They sat in silence as Zeke collected herself. The antique clock ticked loudly. At this hour, the building was empty and it was very quiet. After a few moments, Zeke stopped trembling.

Dr. Taylor sat across from her with a calm reassuring presence. "When you feel ready, why don't you tell me what happened?"

Zeke provided a brief overview without revealing confidential details and explained that her job was to make the informant comfortable enough to do business with another agent. "After we finished lunch, he provided me with the phone numbers we wanted then moved over and put his arm around me. I figured he might do this since I had been flirting, but I wasn't prepared when he actually touched me," Zeke paused and took a deep breath. "When he pulled my hand into his lap and I felt his erection—I freaked. I could see the whole scene when I was attacked and I couldn't get away fast enough." Zeke had pulled her knees up to her chest.

"Tell me what's going on right now."

"I'm really pissed that this happened. I thought I was better and beyond having these damn flashbacks popup without warning. I can't go back to work if this is going to keep happening!"

"I understand you're angry, but you look frightened. What else is going on?"

Zeke looked down and realized that she had curled up in a ball, so she put her feet on the floor. "It isn't just the job, maybe for the first time in my life I have something more important to lose. A relationship with someone really special."

"How do you think this will change your relationship?"

"I'm not the same person as when we met. I feel like two different people, and I'm sure she senses that. I wouldn't want to have to depend on a person who could flip out at any moment. It isn't fair, but I don't want to lose her."

Dr. Taylor crossed her legs and clasped her hands together. "Zeke, it's been about a month since you were brutally assaulted, and I can assure you that virtually no one recovers from that kind of trauma in a month or even two months. This will be a gradual process, and of course, there will be setbacks. What happened to you today was unfortunate because it was essentially another sexual assault and your response was completely appropriate. In fact, you showed incredible self-control in completing your conversation before you left and then debriefed your team. This is one of the reasons they use the term posttraumatic stress disorder. All kinds of everyday occurrences can trigger a response.

"I think you're being overly hard on yourself. It's important that you talk about it with your partner to lessen the power it has on you." She tapped the folder in her lap. "I'm familiar with your need to withhold and maintain control in order to function. Being vulnerable is difficult but integral to your new relationship as well as your self-worth."

Zeke started to interrupt and then stopped. After a moment she said, "I just don't want to drag her into this ugliness."

"And you think withholding something important will create closeness? Zeke, your partner is a mature woman and a nurse. She is also in love with you. I doubt there is much you could say now that would change that."

Zeke thought about Anne's response in the past whenever they had talked about secrets and she knew Dr. Taylor was right.

"Although you seem determined to avoid medications, I'm going to give you a prescription for a mild anti-anxiety medication which will help you, especially at night." She handed Zeke the prescription. "I'd like to see you again on Friday afternoon. And Zeke, if you think it would be beneficial, you are welcome to bring your partner in some time. We can talk about the trauma you have suffered. I would also like you to call the former agent you spoke with to ask about her experiences four weeks after her assault."

Zeke left with the folded prescription in a pocket. She didn't mention the prescription she had received in Chicago. It was apparently in the notes.

†

Zeke started the car and drove as quickly as she could back to the East Mountains. As she climbed through the canyon to the cool air of the higher altitude, the tension seeped out of her body. The flashback had frightened her and revived the monster of self-doubt and fear. Zeke naively believed that the nasty incident was behind her and that she was well on the way to healing. One careless move by a stranger set her back to square one. It helped that Dr. Taylor was able to see her on short notice and provide her with much needed reassurance. Now what she needed most was the warm embrace from her partner.

It was nearly six when Zeke pulled into the driveway then realized that she had never called to say she would be late. *Crap.* She had turned off her cell phone at the doctor's office and just now realized it. She saw Anne feeding the horses and walked over to greet her. "Hey, cowgirl."

Anne looked up from cutting apart the hay bales. "Hi, hon. Glad you're home." She put hay in each of the feeders and swept the loose hay from her jacket and jeans as she walked over to meet Zeke. They kissed while Anne wrapped her arms around Zeke's waist.

Zeke pulled her close and just held her without saying anything.

"Everything okay?" Anne asked.

"I'm okay. Why don't we go inside, it's cold out

169

here." Zeke moved toward the house with her arm around Anne's shoulder. "I have a little surprise for you."

Anne turned down the heat on the pot of homemade soup she had prepared and poured two glasses of wine. Zeke returned after changing into jeans and a hooded sweatshirt and joined Anne on the sofa. "It's good to be home." Zeke pulled Anne close to her and kissed her forehead.

"How did your lunch go? It must have been good if it lasted this long."

Zeke took a deep breath and poured out her story. "It went fine, until the suspect started coming on to me. I freaked out and bolted out of the restaurant. I kept it together until I got my car then I just lost it. I was shaking and hyperventilating; it really scared me."

"My gosh, did he hurt you? What happened?" Anne set down her wineglass onto the table and reached her arm around Zeke's shoulders protectively.

"He didn't do much of anything. He put his arm around me, started whispering, and must have gotten himself all excited because he pulled my hand into his lap and onto his erection. I guess he expected me to do something."

"In the middle of a restaurant?"

"We were in the back of the restaurant and the tablecloth was covering everything, but still it was unexpected and scary." Zeke finished off her wine and put her glass down.

Anne wrapped her other arm around Zeke's waist and held her.

"It took me almost half an hour to get my shit together enough to return to the office. I gave my report and left as quickly as I could. Then the same thing happened when I got to my car. I started shaking and hyperventilating."

"Why didn't you call me? You know I would have come and picked you up."

Zeke kissed her. "I knew you would, baby. But when it happened the second time I thought I better call Dr. Taylor, and fortunately, she was able to see me right away. She talked me down and gently scolded me for thinking I would be cured in a month and for worrying about what you might think."

"Zeke, I understand that feeling vulnerable and scared is difficult for you, it is for most people. It's all the more difficult because you feel that you should somehow have the power to prevent bad things from happening, but none of that has any bearing on my feelings for you and my desire to be close to you. Whenever you have these bad feelings and you keep them inside, it only separates us. I can only love you as much as you let me in."

"Have you been talking to Dr. Taylor?" Zeke smiled realizing she was hearing the same lecture again.

"No, why would you ask?"

"Because, she said almost the same thing. She even offered to have you join us some time."

"I'd like that, if you're willing. What else did she say about today's reaction?"

Zeke sat up a little straighter and took a hold of Anne's hand. "Well, according to the good doctor, what the suspect did was essentially another kind of sexual assault, at least to my psyche. She prescribed medications for me." Zeke noticed that she was holding Anne's hand tightly.

"It's all right, you're okay. I know you're frightened, but it's memories, not real. You're here with me and safe."

They remained snuggled close talking for another

hour until Zeke felt talked out and finally smiled.

While Anne set the table for their dinner, Zeke went upstairs and called Sandra in Tucson. They had a brief conversation in which Sandra reassured Zeke that it was too early to expect miracles. She also advised Zeke to take the rest of her medical leave and when she went back to avoid undercover work for several months. As they talked on the phone, Zeke pulled the small velvet bag from her pocket and examined the delicate gold bracelet. She had intended to give this to Anne when she arrived home. It might be even more meaningful now.

After they finished dinner, Zeke helped clean up the kitchen. When Anne hung up the dishtowel, Zeke wrapped the bracelet around her left wrist and clasped it.

"This is exquisite. Wherever did you find it?"

"I found it in a small boutique before lunch today, and I thought of you which made me happy. I wanted you to know that. I don't tell you often enough how much you have changed my life." Zeke kept holding Anne's hand.

Anne threw her arms around Zeke's neck and kissed her enthusiastically. "You have no idea how much this means to me. Thank you. I will never take it off."

Later, as they climbed into the warm bed, Anne began to talk about her day including the errands and tasks she had completed as she gently stroked Zeke's torso. Zeke pulled her close and kissed her neck, which seemed to be all the invitation Anne needed.

Anne slipped one leg over Zeke as she slid her tee shirt off and began kissing her chest then ran her warm hands along Zeke's sides. When she removed her own tank top and leaned close, their breasts touched lightly.

Her mouth hovered over Zeke's lips then her tongue gently swiped across them.

Zeke felt a sharp electric current shoot down her spine. The touching escalated to an all-consuming desire within minutes. Her hands caressed Anne's thighs and up to her well developed derriere pulling her firmly to her body. Anne began to move her hips rhythmically. Their kisses grew more fervent as their lips meshed and tongues probed.

In a matter of minutes, sensations became jumbled and confused; Zeke could no longer discern the difference between carnal desire and feral rage. She only wanted satisfaction.

Anne responded to her aggression with her own fierceness. Their naked bodies ground together as their kisses became more passionate and hungry. It sometimes seemed that the mere act of love making ignited a deeper fire and longing for oneness and immersion of self. Zeke craved that escape. The intense physical joy they shared was not only exciting but also exhausting. All of Zeke's brain became engaged in her physical body during sex. Her demons could not bother her. They drifted off in each other's arms feeling spent and fulfilled at the same time.

Chapter Fifteen

The backup warning sound of the garbage truck caught her attention. Zeke sipped her coffee and then closed the document on her computer. It was the final copy of her summary from the recent trip to Chicago. Her right knee bounced as she stared at the blank screen trying for the hundredth time, to connect the dots and find the missing piece.

While she was in Chicago with the task force, they had believed that Ahmed Hussein was the major bad actor in the family. She convinced them to look at the brother, Hassan. Zeke pointed out the business and financial activities that had continued even though Ahmed was incommunicado. Someone had been willing to send two armed thugs to find and possibly kill her.

"It's just crazy." She bent over, pulled out a drawer, and propped her feet. Even after she gave up information they wanted, a little voice warned her that they would not give up after one attempt—especially when they realized the information she provided wouldn't help to free him.

Anne was out doing errands and Zeke felt the hairs on the back of her neck standing up as the internal alarms sounded again. Hoping to silence the rising panic, she went downstairs, got a water bottle, and went outside to look around. Her senses heightened as she listened to the routines sounds of trash day—clanging trashcans, a diesel engine, the growl of the compactor, and the backup warning. After clipping her automatic to her waistband, Zeke zipped her jacket and began a random walk through the wooded east side of the property. The fencing was in disrepair and provided limited protection. Yard lights on the house didn't do enough this far way. Motion sensor lights might help, but every animal that went by would activate them.

She glanced back up the hill to the house, which was several hundred feet away. If she wanted access to this house, it would be easy to park off the highway and walk unobserved to the back door. Motion sensors on the house lights would be better. She blamed herself for getting lazy and complacent. *Damn. There is still a threat out there.*

As she stood in the driveway imagining camera locations, Anne drove up. Zeke waved and followed her into the garage. "Welcome home. You know, just as you drove up, I remembered you telling me about someone following you. Has that happened since?"

Anne pulled some bags from the back seat and turned to Zeke. "I'm not sure, but I don't think so."

"Next time we have to go into town, why don't you take my car and I'll have yours checked."

"Do you think something is wrong with it?"

"No, but let's play it safe," Zeke kissed her cheek. "I've spent all morning reviewing the notes from Chicago and I just have a feeling that I'm missing something important."

Anne went inside to change her clothes and Zeke took the opportunity to look under Anne's car. She wasn't surprised to see that there no obvious monitoring device, if they knew she was an agent, they wouldn't try something obvious. The safest plan was to have someone at the office check it out or get rid of the car altogether. Anne was on the phone when Zeke came inside. She watched her as she hung up her jacket and walked through the kitchen past her, and squeezed her arm before heading into the family room.

†

"Yes, I understand, I will—of course, as soon as possible." Anne hung up the phone her hands were shaking slightly.

"Annie? Are you all right?" Zeke's voice sounded like it was in a tunnel.

Anne watched from outside her body as she walked into the family room, staring straight ahead before speaking in an unrecognizable voice. "There's been some kind of accident. My mother—is dead."

Zeke sat stunned.

Anne felt herself thrust into her physical body and began to cry. Hot tears rolled down her face as deep painful sobs wracked her body. Raw emotion poured out as uncorked bottled-up rage. Anne always knew this day would come and envisioned many kinds of responses—fear, anger, grief. But there were no conscious thoughts, no self-pity, no recriminations— just tears.

Zeke quickly wrapped Anne tightly in her arms.

They sat together until Anne drained herself of decades of unshed tears for a relationship that suffered from neglect and misunderstanding.

"I have to go to Arizona."

"Of course. Would you like me to make reservations?"

"Yes, but you don't have to go."

Zeke looked shocked. "Of course I do. I want to be there for you."

"Zeke, there's so much going on there—it's not anything that I'm very proud of and I don't want you to

176

have to endure the family drama."

"Annie, you're my family now. I want to be with you and support you in every way, just as you've done for me."

Anne got up. "I have to pack."

Zeke followed close behind.

"I'll call the airlines. Where are you going? And I'm sure we'll need a rental car." Zeke continued ignoring Anne's attempts to interrupt. "There is no more discussion. I'm going to be at your side regardless of the circumstances, just like you have been for me."

With the reservations made, the bags packed, and the horses looked after, they arrived at the airport in plenty of time for the eight-thirty flight to Phoenix. From there they would drive to Sun City. They had reservations at a nearby motel—where Anne had insisted they stay.

†

Anne's grief manifested itself as agitation, irritability, and sullenness. Everything that Zeke tried irritated her. Anne paced at the airport, wept quietly, and stared out the window for long periods into the dark nothingness that held no answers to her logical and pointless questions. The phone call she had received was from a neighbor who told her he called the police early in the day after a night of screaming and yelling from her mother's home. He hadn't been surprised about the fighting, but after the police arrived, an ambulance followed shortly and transported a body.

She had listened, but a cacophony of cymbals crashing and pounding drums in her head obliterated everything but the fact that her mother was dead.

She was aware of Zeke's presence on the

periphery, but instead of being comforted, she was terrified about allowing Zeke into this dark hole in her life—afraid Zeke would run and she would be left in the dark, alone. She had desperately wanted to share only the sunshine and safe places in Zeke's life, but the reality of her past reared its ugly head.

†

They arrived on time in Phoenix, picked up their luggage, and immediately boarded the shuttle to pick up the rental car. Zeke took charge, secured the luggage, and then fumbled with the map trying to locate their hotel.

In all the rush to reach Sun City and support the fragile grieving woman accompanying her, a distracted Zeke did not notice or recognize the dark-haired man walking out of the rental office to pick up his own luxury Town Car.

†

It was just as Anne remembered. Sun City looked like a rabbit warren with hundreds of small enclaves often grouped around golf courses.

As Zeke navigated the late night traffic onto Interstate 10, Anne began to speak softly and stare out the car window. "My mother and I began to lose touch many years ago when I could no longer deal with her alcoholic behavior. Recently and more frequently, I've received calls from friends and neighbors about her declining health and the erratic disruptive behavior between my mother and her current boyfriend, Brian."

Anne rarely spoke with her estranged mother, but deep inside she knew that one day she would have to

178

deal with her mother's imminent death due to the effects of her alcoholism. She fought hard to keep that dark closet door closed, but over the past few years, her mother's self-destructive lifestyle had become more problematic and public.

Early in the summer, Anne made the drive to the Del Webb Retirement resort outside of Phoenix after she had received a phone call from her mother's neighbors. The phone calls were more frequent as neighbors reacted to the noise and disruption from the Smyth house. Usually a phone call to her mother and or her boyfriend could calm things down for several weeks. But in August, she drove down because her mother was in the hospital with two broken ribs and pneumonia.

Anne had tried to ignore the fact that her seventy-one year old mother had been an alcoholic for most of her life. She had benefited financially from two previous marriages. Before he died, the third husband had the good sense to put the money in trust so that she had limited access. Her mother received a monthly allowance but did not have access to unlimited funds.

After Anne took the job with the University of New Mexico, her mother decided to relocate from Illinois to Arizona thinking they could be closer if they lived in neighboring states. It turned out to be only geographic—their relationship did not improve.

During the recent August trip, she saw her mother's living conditions for the first time in a couple of years and was horrified. The tidy little Del Webb townhouse on the make believe park-like street was cluttered, unkempt, and filthy. After trying to make some order out of chaos for a day and a half, she needed to go to a hotel. She hired an industrial cleaning service to help for the mammoth task and washed her hands of it.

The haze of tobacco smoke, which covered the walls, ceiling, windows, and furniture, obscured the superficial clutter of dirty dishes, overflowing laundry baskets, and unwashed linens. In every room, there were overflowing ashtrays and beer cans. At first, Anne could only walk from room to room with a trash bag shaking her head. The current boyfriend was conveniently out of town when she arrived, or so her mother told her. And that made it easier to accomplish the job without interference.

Each day she worked alongside the cleaning crew by throwing out items she felt were beyond hope, including most of the linens, several broken glasses, dishes, and numerous burned pots and pans. She also went through the cupboards pitching hidden bottles and unusable food packages.

In the evening, she would visit her mother at the hospital and try yet again, to convince her mother to accept some treatment—she adamantly refused. She insisted that she and Brian were just fine without any help.

When Anne had a chance to talk with the doctor, he explained that this was only one of several admissions she had over the past year. He strongly suspected her mother of being abused, but could not actually prove it without her testimony.

Both Marjorie and Brian behaved, for the entire world, like a very happy couple.

Anne had met Brian, three years earlier when he showed up at a holiday mixer at the resort and began courting her mother. It was obvious to her friends in the community that the man was penniless and looking for a widow to take care of him. Before hearing that, Anne had felt uncomfortable with his smarmy, phony affectionate behavior and inability to make eye contact. His appearance was that of an aging movie star with dark shifty eyes, slicked black-dyed hair, and a cloying southern accent. On closer examination, his suits were old and worn; his starched white shirts had greasy collars and cuffs and his fingernails were never clean. Anne didn't trust him and she didn't like him but her mother captivated by his charm, gushed because he was so 'romantic'.

Anne elected to stay away from them both for her own mental health.

After settling her mother into her cleaner home with her promises to stop the drinking and take better care of herself, Anne returned to New Mexico with the fear that there would be another trip sooner than later.

Anne turned away from the window and looked at Zeke. "Last night's phone call from their neighbor, telling me he had to call the police and they removed a body from the house…" She choked on the word and sobbed for several moments before regaining composure enough to finish. "…and that Brian was arrested. It's—the end of a tragic story."

The war with her mother was over, and Anne was now alone. They had remained locked in a struggle for years pushing against each other and now Anne found herself teetering on a precipice without the constant resistance to which she was accustomed. It was a scary place and she was frightened.

†

Zeke simply reached out and placed her hand on the back of Anne's neck. They continued in silence as Zeke tried to absorb what she had learned. What could she possibly say? It was a nightmare. Zeke swallowed hard, took Anne's hand, and briefly thought about her own mother's health. How long before she would get the same phone call.

She thought she had a reasonably good profile of Anne, the woman with whom she shared her life, but clearly still waters run deep and peeling back layers of history took time and patience. Still, her heart ached for the pain that her lover was enduring and she felt twinges from the recent losses in her life.

It was a little after ten p.m. when they settled into their room at the hotel. The facility was new, clean, and most of all, quiet. It was centrally located between her mother's house and the police department.

Zeke unpacked while Anne made a call to the local police.

After she hung up, Anne looked around the room, as if lost. "Zeke?"

"I'm right here." Zeke crossed the room quickly as Anne began to sway. She gently sat Anne on the bed and held her. "It's okay, I'm here, shhh."

"They said there was nothing I could do. The case is a possible homicide. How could that be? They were talking about my mother—that someone may have killed her—they're waiting on autopsy results before charging Brian. I don't understand."

"You can't do anything tonight. We'll go first thing in the morning. Take a deep breath; it's okay." Zeke got up and crossed to the small refrigerator and unlocked the mini bar, grabbed a small bottle of whiskey and poured it into a glass. Handing it to Anne, she said, "Take a sip."

Anne obeyed, and when she put the empty glass down, she no longer trembled.

Zeke removed her shoes. "You need to rest now, let's take off those clothes and get you into bed."

Anne allowed Zeke to help her into the clean white sheets where she curled into a fetal position as the voluminous comforter swallowed her.

Zeke tidied up the room then joined Anne. Muffled sobs were the only sounds Zeke heard throughout the night.

†

Although she cried most of the night, Anne felt a little more focused after a good night's sleep. It was a short drive to the Sun City Police Department. There was no new information from what they heard the night before and the arresting officer was not on duty yet. A young detective led them down several hallways until they reached a large black and white sign that said morgue.

"We're on hold until you identify the body. The medical examiner has finished, but we couldn't release the body until you arrived and gave us some information."

There were several metal folding chairs against the one industrial green wall and a large curtained window next to the door.

"If you could just wait here a minute," he said.

They took a seat while the young man with blond curly hair went through the double doors, sending a cloud of dank, refrigerated air into the hallway.

"Are you okay, Annie?"

She heard Zeke's voice, nodded, and reached for Zeke's hand.

It was several minutes before the detective returned to ask if Anne would rather view the body or make the ID through the window.

With no hesitation, she stood and walked through

the double stainless steel doors and into the viewing room. It was another small room with the same nauseating industrial green paint. A white-sheeted stainless steel gurney stood in the center of the room. The walls were bare.

The morgue attendant stood at attention next to the body. Anne reached for Zeke's hand then nodded as he carefully folded back the sheet to the shoulders. Anne's knees buckled, and she swayed. She covered her mouth to keep her shock and sorrow from escaping and spilling out.

The attendant and the detective left the room leaving the two of them alone with Anne's mother.

The odors assaulted her nose—formaldehyde and Pine Sol hung in the refrigerated air. She moved closer staring at her mother's pale silent face. The previously tormented woman looked peaceful—more than she had in years. Anne's heart ached thinking that the only path to peace had to be death.

She slowly traced her fingers across her mom's smooth, cold cheek. The sculpted cheekbones, elegant nose, and the perfectly shaped lips reminded Anne of the beautiful woman her mother had once been. Soft waves of salt and pepper hair surrounded her colorless face. For years, she sought out that face in times of happiness, sadness, and fear. Her mother raised her and provided her with the foundation she would need. Anne grew up with discipline and a great deal of unconditional love. Sadness swept over her like a stinging wave of cold water.

Like an old silent movie, scenes from her youth flashed in jerky black and white pictures across her mind. Girl scouts—holiday meals—report cards—her first bike—her first heartbreak—the absence of her father. Interspersed was the memory of the warmth of her mother's arms and the sound of her laughter. She ached knowing she would never feel that joy of motherhood again.

Anne stared at the inanimate face trying to memorize every feature. After this moment, she would never see her mother again, and she wanted to remember.

She let out a small gasp when she pulled the sheet down a little further and saw dark purple marks around her neck accentuated by the grey-white skin. If what the police suspected was true—this was not a peaceful ending.

Anne choked back a sob, and then she leaned down and kissed her mother's cold cheek for the last time.

†

They sat silently in the sun-baked car for twenty minutes until Anne stopped shivering and could give Zeke directions to the house her mother owned in the Del Webb Retirement community.

"Just turn right on West Bell Avenue and keep going to 91st street."

"Are you sure you're up to this?" Zeke asked. She steered the car onto the wide thoroughfare.

"I don't know. I just want to get this over with as soon as possible."

"Would you like me to stop and pick up something to eat?"

"I'm not hungry. We can get something later. Turn here." Anne pointed to her right. "When you reach Tumblewood, turn right again."

The closer they got, the more scared Anne became. Her pulse was racing and the earlier chills seemed more like a cold sweat. It was like returning to the scene of a crime. In this case, the crime scene was her mother's murder. Anne hugged her arms tightly around herself.

"Take this first right, its 91st Drive. It turns into West Kathleen Road. Mom's house is halfway down the block on the left." The semi familiar neighborhood felt eerily quiet. The neighbors weren't outside tending their yards, which they often were. It looked deserted. "Pull in here."

Zeke parked in the wide driveway in front of a three-car garage, which occupied the majority of space for the house. She switched off the engine and looked around. "This would be a hard place to find without perfect directions. Every house is identical. Amazing."

The best Anne could do was to stare at the beige garage door and will her body to move. Her mind was spinning with terrifying visions of what she might find when she opened the front door. She glanced quickly at Zeke. "Promise you'll stay with me."

"I promise. Are you sure, you want to do this now? There's no hurry. We can come back tomorrow if you'd rather."

Looking at Zeke's strong face, Anne felt a surge of confidence. "I'm sure. Let's go."

The yellow tape across the front door read "Crime Scene Do Not Enter". Anne looked at Zeke unsure what to do. Fear, embarrassment, and creeping rage inflamed raw nerves and caused her hands to clench.

"It's okay, they released the body. The detective said we could go in, they've finished."

Anne felt dizzy, her mind raced with horrifying thoughts about the condition of the house. It had been months since she had the industrial cleaning done, and she was mortified about what Zeke would think about the condition of the house and, by association, how she would be judged. "Zeke, I don't know how much time you've spent in homes of alcoholics—but they can be pretty awful."

"Annie, this has nothing to do with you. Remember, I spent several months undercover as a vagrant—no bathing, no clean clothes, no house. Whatever you're worried about, I've seen worse. We'll do this together." She squeezed Anne's hand.

The house and yard looked quiet and neat as they walked to the door. Nearby, curtains parted in houses of curious neighbors. As Anne cautiously opened the door, the smell of stale cigarette smoke and garbage assaulted her. The house was cool, dark, and silent as a tomb. The hot Arizona sun had not penetrated the interior of this house for years. Stacks of magazines, newspapers, and circulars covered the floors.

Litter including mail, overflowing ashtrays, empty beer bottles, and dishes, obscured all horizontal surfaces. Anne, suddenly claustrophobic, moved quickly across the living room to the rear dining room and pulled back the vertical blinds, opened the patio doors wide, and stood there unmoving. Her mind was teetering on the edge of reality. An electric jolt shot through her body when she thought of her mother murdered in this house. Her knees started to buckle. She forced herself into the present and moved into robot mode. "Well, no use standing around, I have a lot to do."

"If that's what you want to do, I'll do whatever you need. What's your plan?"

"I'll need to clean it out and sell it. My mother made that much clear to me. She put the deed in my name the last time I was here. She left nothing for Brian. She was angry with him, but not ready to kick him out—she still needed a drinking buddy." Anne spat the last words angrily.

"What do you want to keep and what can be discarded?" Zeke took off her jacket.

Anne's shoulders sagged. "I don't know."

They spent the next five hours sorting and bagging.

Anne found most of her mother's jewelry—nothing too valuable. The walk-in closet was in shambles and not worth sorting. Everything went into large plastic garbage bags.

There were a few picture albums and a box of photo envelopes, which Zeke dutifully placed in the car. Anne quickly sorted the piles of mail into important and junk—there was nothing with Brian's name. He had very few personal belongings—all of which they bagged and labeled.

By late afternoon, Anne was shaking from exhaustion and hunger.

"Why don't we call it a day and come back tomorrow?" asked Zeke.

Anne simply nodded. Small talk required too much energy. The only things she could handle were tasks. Her body was on auto-pilot. Every object in her path went to one of three places—keep—sell—trash. Zeke locked the house, poured Anne into the car, and drove them back to the motel.

†

Anne simply followed directions. They each took a hot soapy shower to remove the sweat and stench. After dressing in some casual clothes, Zeke suggested they go down to the pool bar for a drink.

Zeke brought two Piña coladas to the lounge chairs near the pool where Anne stretched out in the fall sunshine.

"This might be just what the doctor ordered." Zeke

handed the fancy drink to Anne.

"This looks wonderful," Anne said. "And it tastes even better."

"Slow down there, missy, you haven't eaten and you might end up getting pretty hammered." Zeke smiled.

"So what. It just might help. It certainly worked for my mom." Sarcasm prickled the air as hot salty tears cascaded down her cheeks without warning.

Zeke made no response.

Along with several hors d'ouvres, they sipped Piña coladas until the sun went down then slowly made their way to their room.

The wildly fluctuating emotions fueled by good quality rum made Anne feel as though she had gone six rounds with a mechanical bull.

The room was comfortable, cool, and quiet and they stretched out on the bed and talked.

Zeke rolled up on her side and doubled a pillow under her head. "When you were younger, were you and your mother closer?"

Anne closed her eyes and a vision of a long ago Christmas appeared. "Yeah, we were. After my dad left, she focused on my needs. It was almost as though she felt she had to work twice as hard to make up for his absence. It was nice. She never missed an event at school and my friends thought she was the best mother in the world. They loved coming over to my house. Anne reached for Zeke's hand. "That all changed during my junior year in high school. I don't know what happened. She never talked about it, but I'm pretty sure that's when she started drinking. By the time I graduated, she had begun dating. I had a really hard time with that, but she brushed me off whenever I complained. I went away to nursing school and spent less and less time at home."

Her muscles were completely relaxed, but Anne felt the familiar tightening in her chest.

"That's when she remarried for the first time. I was excited because I thought she would settle down and be happy. It lasted six months." Anne laughed mirthlessly. "She had good taste and married two others, both rich. One was divorced, and the second died. That's when she moved to Arizona. I hoped that a change of scenery would make a difference." Her voice cracked with emotion. "It made a difference all right."

Anne's deep hurt and anger surfaced with a vengeance. The muscles in her jaw tightened and a cold knot formed in the pit of her stomach. She felt betrayed and abandoned. In spite of the past animosity and recriminations, she was not ready to be without a mother—her mother. Anne began to weep at her loss, and at the same time, railed at her mother with her next breath. "How could she do this to me? She was too young to die and I'm too young to be without my mother! It isn't fair."

"I know, Annie. You're right, this never should've happened." Zeke pulled her close until the emotional storm subsided and Anne nodded off for a short time.

Anne awoke to a strange noise in the room. The clock radio said eight-fifteen and it was dark out. The smell of food caused her to sit up and she found that Zeke had ordered room service—two hamburgers along with some soup, all of which smelled delicious. "What a good idea. I think my appetite's back. You take such good care of me."

"You're important to me and I want to take care of you. We both worked hard today and we'll need the calories to finish the job. Are you feeling a little better?"

"Yes. I guess I was more tired than I thought I was. And I'm sorry to drag you into this nightmare."

"I want to always be at your side, no matter what." Zeke kissed her forehead and led her over to the small table.

Anne inhaled the food barely tasting it, but it seemed to fill a hole in her. She watched Zeke eating and felt a tug in her heart for the wonderful woman willing to share her joy and pain. "I'm so glad I didn't have to do this alone. You've been so wonderfully supportive. You have no idea how much it means to me. Whatever crises I've had in my life, I've always had to handle it alone. It's so different to have someone with me every step of the way, loving me through it."

Zeke reached across the small table and took her hand. "I know exactly what you mean because you have done the same thing for me. On more than one occasion, I might add."

A surge of warmth flooded her body. Anne stood up. "Make love to me, please. Take me out of this hell for a little while and make me feel nothing but pleasure. Please, Zeke, will you do that? "

Zeke reached for her outstretched hand, pulled her close, and captured her mouth with a fierce, ravaging kiss.

Anne surrendered all of her thoughts to her physical desire and willed herself into sexual oblivion at the hands of her lover.

Chapter Sixteen

They spent the next two days in the methodical deconstruction of the former house of pain, as they dubbed it. They sorted, boxed, bagged, and trashed every single item in the house. Anything worth donating went to some charity until all that remained was unsalvageable junk. Local haulers came to remove everything else that remained, including the carpeting.

Late Monday afternoon, Anne received a call a call from the funeral home telling her that her mother's ashes were ready. By the third day, they were standing in a completely vacant house ready for professionally cleaning and painting.

Anne called her mother's lawyer to be sure there were no surprises—there weren't. Next, they found a realtor who assured her that there should be no trouble selling the home since this was such a desirable community.

Throughout the purging and cleaning, not one person came by or called. When the Real Estate sign appeared in the yard, the next-door neighbor, the same neighbor who regularly made the phone calls to Anne, came out with her husband. "Hello Ms. Reynolds, you remember my husband Tom. I am so sorry about this terrible tragedy. You know how much I liked your mother, and this was just so unfortunate."

Anne flashed anger and her neck muscles tightened, immediately thinking that if the neighbor had really cared about her mother she should have done something sooner, something that would have altered the present reality. She fisted her hands in the pockets of her jeans and stifled her anger. In reality, she knew there wasn't anything neighbors could have done to prevent this train wreck. "I know, I appreciate your keeping in touch the way you did."

"Are you planning a service here?" asked the woman.

"No, actually, I was just going to take the ashes home with me. I didn't plan a service." Anne never even thought about a funeral. She was convinced that her mother had no social life or friends anymore.

"Of course, you need to follow your mother's wishes and she certainly abhorred funerals. She made that very clear."

That was news to Anne.

"Well, we just wanted to offer our condolences. I'm sure you have a lot to do. Goodbye, Ms. Reynolds."

They were gone and Anne went back inside to find Zeke who was taking one last walk through looking for anything they might have missed. She said nothing but walked into Zeke's arms and held on to her tightly.

The attorney would handle the legal work and he would call as it progressed. The police charged Brian with involuntary manslaughter since they had no proof of premeditation. The neighbors would likely be called if they needed any more evidence, but the numerous police reports and Brian's apparent lack of denial would likely lead to a conviction. There was nothing more Anne could do for her murdered mother in Sun City, Arizona.

†

By late afternoon on Tuesday, they were packed and heading to the Mountain West Regional Airport, thereby avoiding the larger hub and more unnecessary stress. There wasn't much Zeke could do, just be supportive. Sadness filled the wordless silence. Anne had little to say, clearly dealing with the events of the past week. And while they distanced themselves from the pain in Sun City and closer to the airport and home, Anne would frequently reach out to touch Zeke for comfort.

"You know what I'd like to do? I'd like to run away, someplace where no one knows us, a desert island in the middle of the ocean where we could just lie around all day and do nothing." Anne smiled, for the first time in days. "We could act silly, eat bananas off the trees, drink rum punch's, and swim naked in the ocean."

"There's no reason why we can't do that. When we get home, I'll do a little research and we'll figure a way to run away together, okay?"

"Are you serious? I would love it. Let's do it. I can't wait. I just want to be alone with you every minute of every day." Anne wrapped her arms around Zeke's neck and kissed her.

"Sure we can, why not. We both could use a break." Zeke turned down the next street and followed the signs to the rental return lot in an industrial looking area west of the airport. She pulled into the large car rental lot and found an empty spot in the area marked for returned cars. "I'll get the bags out. I think we just passed one of the shuttle vans so it shouldn't be too long."

Anne waited with Zeke. The white courtesy minivan pulled up as Zeke closed the trunk.

The driver, a thin dark haired man with a brand new ill-fitting uniform, opened the tailgate of the van.

"Good afternoon ma'am, just these two bags?" He

lifted their suitcases into the back of the van. Zeke cringed as she thought about the brass urn containing the ashes from the funeral home.

Anne climbed into the middle seat and Zeke followed.

He latched the side door, went around to the driver's side, and drove a little further down the aisle. Zeke buckled her seat belt and squeezed Anne's arm. "You okay?" Anne just nodded and rested her head against the van window. There were no clever words to console her. "It won't be long now." Zeke's attention turned to the van's driver. *It's curious that he hasn't called in to report picking up two new passengers.*

The driver slowed as they reached the end of the aisle. Zeke watched as a thin middle-aged man wearing a yellow Hawaiian shirt, a red Cardinals baseball cap, and sunglasses waved. He picked up a backpack with an Arizona cardinals logo on it. Once they had stopped, the driver got out, spoke a few words to the man, and opened the side door. "This gentleman is also departing."

The new arrival excused himself and moved to the rear seat

The van continued down the aisle. The stranger behind them rustled in his backpack, leaned forward, and spoke in a low accented voice. "We meet again, Special Agent Cabot."

Zeke heard Anne gasp and turned enough to see an automatic with a silencer behind Anne's ear with the stranger's other hand circling Anne's throat.

"Do not turn around and do not move or I will kill your friend."

Shit. Her mind raced. She looked at the driver hopefully, but he smiled in his rearview mirror. They were on their own. "What do you want?" She spoke as calmly as possible. Beside her, Anne trembled; her face was pale and pinched.

"I think you know the answer. I want to know where my brother is being held and I want the truth."

Zeke could hear the barely contained anger resonating in his voice. *Hassan Hussein! God, Dammit.* Adrenalin surged through her bloodstream. Options scrolled through her brain faster than she could process them. *Stay calm and don't piss him off.*

"As I told Mr. Mubarak's 'errand boys', your brother was arrested because of his federal indictment for murder. Look, the CIA intervened with new evidence. They said that because of the Patriot Act, an affiliation with a terrorist makes him an enemy combatant."

Hassan pushed the gun against Anne's head. "I am not fucking around with you." he shouted. "Tell me where he is or I will kill her." He grabbed Anne's hair pulling her up in the seat causing her to scream.

"Stop! Listen, I'm telling you the truth. He's at Guantanamo Bay," Zeke yelled.

He shoved the gun against Zeke's temple while maintaining a grip on Anne's hair. "I know what you told the men we sent to find you. My lawyers spent a week on your damn lie. They even flew to Cuba two weeks ago. No Ahmed Hussein was registered there." His eyes were wild with rage and the gun barrel jabbed her head as his hand trembled.

"Wait. I don't understand. I was in the interrogation room when the CIA agent told us they were leaving immediately for Gitmo for further interrogation—and they left with him. Look, let us go. I promise I'll make a phone call and find out where he is."

The driver interrupted. "The car—your car is here

to pick us up, boss, we gotta get out of here."

"I warn you, this is your last chance. I'll hold you to that promise, Agent Cabot. Tie them up." He edged past with the gun still trained on Anne's head.

The driver had hurried around and slid open the door allowing Hussein to back out. He quickly tied Anne's hands to the driver seat headrest in front of her and then duct-taped her mouth.

Zeke watched frantically as Hassan turned the gun on her. Behind him, the passenger door of a black sedan stood open.

The driver was furiously wrapping her wrists with a nylon cord and over his shoulder; Zeke could see Hassan backing into the sedan. Once he was inside and they were no longer in his line of sight, she head-butted the man in holding her wrists and used her half-tied hands to shove him out the open door.

He yelped as he hit the pavement and Zeke furiously pulled her hands free and grabbed for the weapon under her jacket.

The men in the sedan were yelling, 'get in the car' and a hand reached out to him as the car started to move.

Weapon in hand, she yanked the seat belt off and charged out of the car as the black sedan sped off. She fired rapidly and watched three shots strike the back of the vehicle as the car turned toward the exit. She ran between the next rows of cars but the sedan was gone. She hurried back to the van and dialed 911. "Annie hang on, I'll get you free. This is Special Agent Cabot, send a unit to parking lot A at the Mountain West Regional Airport, for a shooting, and notify the FBI."

She worked the knots loose as she spoke, and then gently removed the duct tape. "Are you okay?"

Anne clung to her. "Yes, I'm fine. Are you okay?

Did they hurt you?"

"I'm fine, but I couldn't catch them, they're gone." Zeke reholstered her weapon, climbed out, and walked to the rear of the van. Her hands shook with the rage and her jaw ached from her tight facial muscles. She dialed the number for the Chicago office and left a message.

Anne joined her behind the van. "I didn't want to stay in there by myself." She still looked pale and trembled. "Zeke, I'm scared."

"I know, Annie, help is on the way." Zeke hugged her close. Her gut tightened. *When is this damn nightmare going to end?* Zeke's addled brain was incapable of processing the whole scene and was relieved to see the flashing lights and sirens grow closer.

Zeke gave a full report to the responding police officer and asked if they had called the local FBI office. She provided a full description of Hassan Hussein as well as what little she could remember of the driver. She was certain that by now Hussein had disappeared again.

A local FBI agent named Henderson showed up ten minutes later and took Zeke aside where she explained the situation so they could issue an alert for the suspects. This was the second assault on a federal officer ordered by Hassan Hussein.

The local police cordoned off the area while Zeke and Anne sat in the car with Agent Henderson. He offered to get their luggage and then would transport them to his office.

Zeke took Anne's hand. "I'm so sorry. I feel like I've dragged you into a really horrible situation that has nothing to do with you and I don't know how to make it right." Overwhelmed with guilt, anger, and pain, her voice broke.

"We can sort it all out later. I just want to go home. I don't have any more energy to think, feel, or even worry. Please just get me out of here."

"I promise, as soon as we finish the paperwork will be on our way home."

Two hours later, the paperwork was complete, Zeke's service weapon confiscated as evidence, and a new one issued. Agent Henderson changed their reservation and drove them to the Airport.

✝

Zeke found a seat for Anne then went to the ticket counter to check on the flight to Albuquerque. When she handed the ticket agent her credit card and ID, a light bulb went off in Zeke's head. She had used 'her' credit card to pay for the plane tickets, motel and rental car. If someone wanted to find her, the easiest way was through her credit card. *Son of a bitch.* What could she have possibly been thinking? *Shit.* She risked both of their lives because of sheer carelessness. Her stomach clenched and she felt another wave of nausea resulting from shame and embarrassment. She glanced over her shoulder to see Anne seated on a bench near the window with the luggage. The overhead lights framed Anne's face as she rested her head against the window. Her normally strong shoulders bowed under the weight of her grief and pain.

Zeke felt sick and responsible for Anne's pain. Her heart ached for the amazingly resilient woman. There had to be some way to right this wrong. She leaned back on the ticket counter as fatigue threatened. Every muscle in her body hurt from days of overuse, her head pounded, and the edges of terror threatened her last vestige of self-respect. This could very well be the last blow to her career.

Chapter Seventeen

The next day passed with little conversation as each woman wrestled with her own demons. Zeke kept a close eye on Anne but respected her request to be alone.

Anger was a powerful motivator. Her sexual assault several weeks ago had shut her down and rendered her powerless. This attack on Anne enraged her and the fear of further retribution from this elusive lunatic frightened her. The best medicine would be for her to focus all that energy on something productive instead of ruminating.

Zeke withdrew to recheck her notes. She still couldn't believe what Hassan had told her. *He has to be at Gitmo, where else could he be?* It was still early afternoon in Chicago when she decided to call Special Agent in Charge Frank Hartbrooke. He was still in charge of the Hussein case and wanted her to keep in touch. His secretary recorded her number and message. SAC Hartbrooke called back within ten minutes.

"Good morning, Agent Cabot. I'm glad you called because I got your message last night."

"Good morning, sir. I wasn't sure how long the full report might take. I thought I'd give you my version."

"All right, you have my attention."

"I was returning from a quick trip to Arizona with a friend because of the sudden death of her mother."

"I'm sorry. Always a difficult situation, I'm sure."

"Yes. When we returned the rental car on Tuesday afternoon, two men abducted us in a courtesy van, held us at gunpoint, and then tied us up. I was able to intervene and got several shots off before I lost them. It was Hassan Hussein. I gave him the information he wanted—the location of his brother—I thought that was Gitmo. He claimed that his lawyers went to Cuba two weeks ago and Ahmed Hussein was not there. I told him to let us go and I would try to find out, he did and swore to hold me to my promise."

"This kind of escalation bothers me. Like you, I assumed the report was accurate. I'll try to find out if the CIA director can shed any light on this. You gave all this to Henderson and the local cops?"

"Yes sir, the local police are looking for Hassan and the accomplice, and the Phoenix FBI office has the details. I wanted to call you myself to see if you knew what was going on."

"As you know, these folks have some powerful and wealthy resources available to them and seem quite determined. Not many people can access those records. How do you think they tracked you to Arizona?"

Zeke had hoped he wouldn't ask her and swallowed hard. "I'm afraid that was my fault, sir. In the rush to help my friend, I offered to make the plane, hotel and car reservations—in my name with my old credit card."

There was a brief but icy silence. "I'm surprised and a very disappointed, Agent Cabot, especially since you knew that your identity was already compromised from the earlier assault."

"It was a serious error in judgment, sir. I will report it to the local SAC on Monday and prepare for an OPR hearing."

"The Office of Professional Responsibility can wait. I'd rather have you work with Agent Donovan right now. His experience will be more helpful.

Besides, you are still technically on medical leave—although, it seems to be a very active medical leave."

Zeke smiled at his reference to how much trouble she had been during her leave.

They hung up with a promise to stay in touch. She walked into the bedroom where Anne was napping and sat on the settee near the window to watch her exhausted lover sleep. Anne's blond curls fell across her forehead and the side of her face. Her left hand tucked under her chin, and her knees folded up tightly. Zeke felt her heart squeeze as she thought about the overwhelming shock and grief that Anne had to process.

The medical examiner's final report cited the primary cause of her mother's death as a homicide by strangulation. The secondary findings of healed fractures and recent bruising were consistent with a long history of physical abuse. Anne had taken the news personally and blamed herself for having missed the clues.

Chronic abuse cases were not new to Zeke. Violence perpetrated on women and children by men, so easily capable of overpowering them, remained a hot button issue for Zeke. Even more so now. In the past, solving those types of crimes had brought her a particular satisfaction.

As she watched the vulnerable woman sleep, it saddened her to think that Anne had felt it necessary to keep her mother's history a secret. Once again, Zeke felt as though she were at fault since Anne didn't feel safe enough to open up and chose instead to keep her past shrouded in darkness. She looked like a fragile woman sleeping and not the strong, vital person she had become. Anne was the one who successfully captured Zeke's heart. She bent over and gently kissed the top of

Anne's head and whispered, "I love you, Annie."

Zeke slipped out of the bedroom, closed the door, and went downstairs to call Dr. Taylor for a follow-up appointment. This time she wanted Anne to go with her.

Later, Zeke returned to the bedroom with coffee and toast.

Anne smiled as she entered.

"Good morning, beautiful." Zeke set the plate on the bedside table.

"What time is it? I didn't mean to sleep so long." Anne sat up and leaned against the headboard as her sheer nightgown slid low over her breasts.

"After eleven, thought you might be hungry. There's no reason in the world for you to get up. Is there anything I could help you with?" Zeke stroked her leg lightly.

Anne sipped her coffee and smiled. "No. You're right. Let's both stay in bed all day."

"We can do that. Would you rather skip the event at the art gallery in Santa Fe tonight?"

"Oh crap, I completely forgot about that. No, I really want to dress up and enjoy a night out on the town."

"We don't have to decide right now. We can see how you feel later." Zeke stretched out next to her lover and kissed her.

†

Later Saturday afternoon, the attractive couple was dressed and pressed in their finest, en route to the gala event. Zeke grinned recalling the vision of Anne as she walked regally down the stairs at the house in a deep rust and gold-colored dress with her hair loosely pinned up.

The hour-long drive up the Turquoise Trail gave them a chance to enjoy each other's company and a beautiful Saturday afternoon. The endless blue sky had only an occasional cumulus cloud to mar the expanse. Mild forty degree temperatures were comfortable as the afternoon sun shone through the sunroof. When they pulled up to the museum door, a young man came up to the driver's side of the car. "Valet, ma'am?"

"Yes, thanks." He held the doors as both exited the car. They approached the Georgia O'Keefe museum, an unassuming one-story adobe building where the receiving line spilled out the front door. Zeke felt underdressed compared to the well-heeled crowd of Santa Fe's rich and famous schmoozing with one another.

Anne whispered and pointed out some political types with whom she had once socialized. Several of them recognized the former wife of the disgraced Albuquerque City Councilman Andrew Reynolds and greeted her with plastic smiles.

"Lordy, there'll be tongues wagging within minutes. I hope that the 'grapevine' filters the news back to Andrew that his ex-wife made an appearance on the arm of a stunning woman." Anne smiled and laughed. "He's 'so' fond of you."

Once inside, each sponsor introduced him or herself. Anne leaned into Zeke. "Keep your eye on the attractive woman we're approaching."

She needn't have bothered as Zeke received warm welcome by the incomparable Amanda Joy Lujan, who carefully looked her over as if evaluating a new horse.

"Well that was odd." Zeke looked back over her shoulder as the hostess winked at her.

"Not really. From what I've heard, Amanda Joy

has some very special soirees with a select group of people which is hush-hush." Anne directed Zeke away from the door and toward the bar.

Since they agreed it would be a long night, they'd skip the alcohol. "Two tonics with lime." Zeke accepted two glasses and handed one to Anne. "Thank you."

They wandered through the exhibit chatting happily together and admiring O'Keefe's works. Anne provided interesting history and background that she had gleaned from previous visits.

Zeke, of course, recognized O'Keefe's work. She knew little about the history surrounding her extraordinary life. Hearing the stories and having seen the rich and varied landscape of New Mexico, made the paintings more alive and meaningful. Although she never believed herself to be an art enthusiast, Zeke admitted the evocative paintings of the desert caused a visceral response that was both sensuous and relaxing. She made a mental note to plan a trip to Abiquiu with Anne. She wanted to understand more about the allure of the vast high desert in that area.

Anne hovered closely taking every opportunity to touch or lean against Zeke.

Zeke watched the sideways glances from curious guests. She realized this event might be the first local outing for Anne. Even in a community as liberal as Santa Fe, Zeke recognized the whispered speculations.

More than once Anne commented about the people watching them—especially the blatant admiration from Amanda Joy.

Zeke's guard suddenly clicked on. This reminded her of a high society job in New York. Here she was rubbing elbows with the gentrified city folk and the few Hollywood celebrities who had taken up residence in

New Mexico. It triggered her normal agency radar. Although there were no specific stand-outs, her senses were heightened and on alert. Social events meant crowds of unsuspecting people milling about providing a diversion for anyone with an agenda. Zeke was on guard for danger. She had underestimated potential threats recently, and this time she would be ready. Her hand slid under her jacket and touched the comfort of her weapon securely tucked under her left arm.

"Would you hold this while I run to the ladies room?" Anne handed Zeke her glass.

†

Anne had excused herself for the restroom, where she stood staring at herself in the mirror while she washed her hands. Other than being a little pale, Anne admired the glow of a woman who was clearly in love. That look had been absent for too many years. Dressing up was something she missed. Tonight, the glow seemed obvious to her and probably to others as well. She was determined to enjoy herself and put the past week behind her—at least for now. The creamy bronze lipstick she applied helped accentuate a glow in her cheeks and she then adjusted a loose wave in her hair.

Zeke had cautioned her that it might feel awkward publicly acknowledging her relationship with another woman. On the contrary, it was exciting and curiously, she didn't feel awkward or uncomfortable. So much had happened between them in the past few weeks that she could scarcely remember a time when Zeke was not a part of her life. In spite of the harrowing trials, sharing those times with Zeke had been a positive experience. She smiled just thinking about her stunning lover and blushed slightly at the arousal just thinking

207

about the physical passion they shared.

When she returned to the gallery, she searched for Zeke and noticed a woman sitting nearby who looked familiar. "Dr. Stone?" she asked.

The woman turned and stood up. "Yes, I'm sorry. I'm not very good at names."

"I'm Anne Reynolds, well it was Lindbergh then. I was the head nurse in the OR several years ago." Anne reached out her hand.

The doctor seemed a little older than Anne remembered with a smattering of gray at her temples, but there was no mistaking the kind face and warm hazel eyes.

"Of course, I remember you, an excellent head nurse. It's nice to see you again. We certainly missed you after you left. What are you doing now?"

"I work part time in home health nursing, just to maintain my skills." Anne smiled. "I have to tell you that I promised myself if I ever needed surgery, you would be the person I would call because I admired your skill so much. Fortunately, I have remained healthy, but I have your number just in case."

Dr. Stone smiled and blushed slightly.

Zeke walked up interrupting their conversation.

"Dr. Stone, I'd like you to meet my—friend, Zeke Cabot." Now it was Anne's turn to blush.

They shared a moment of recognition, and Zeke smiled as she put out her hand. "Dr. Stone."

"Please call me, Sam." She shook Zeke's hand. "It's nice to meet you. Are you a nurse, as well?"

"No, unfortunately. I work as a federal agent."

"How interesting. Did you two meet recently? I seem to remember Anne, you were married—a lawyer wasn't it?"

"You're correct, but that's a long story for another

time. Zeke and I met a couple of months ago. I had to rescue her when she injured herself while hiking, a horrible incident with a dangerous snake." Anne looked at Zeke and grinned.

An attractive woman joined them and casually draped her arm around Dr. Stone's shoulders. "Hi, am I too late to join the party?"

"Of course not," said Sam. "This is Gloria. Honey, I'd like you to meet Anne Reynolds, a former coworker and her friend, Zeke Cabot."

Anne slowly connected the dots. *Dr. Stone's girlfriend.* She never would've guessed. *Huh, see I do know a lesbian.* The woman was drop dead gorgeous. She was taller than Dr. Stone was with lustrous olive skin, a mane of shiny black hair, and a sensational figure. *So much for stereotypes.*

The conversation flowed naturally as Sam and Anne recalled current employees they both knew that worked at the hospital.

Gloria and Zeke fell comfortably into their own conversation and Gloria wasted no time exploring Zeke's FBI background.

Anne tried to eavesdrop as Gloria questioned Zeke. It seemed the two strangers shared similar memories of time spent in New York. They compared notes on favorite attractions and eateries.

Sam and Anne left to refresh the drinks while Zeke and Gloria offered to find a table. It was late when Zeke suggested they start their long drive home.

"I sympathize with you," Sam said. "We have a reservation at La Fonda for tonight, just because I didn't want to make that drive. I'm sure you could get a room if you wanted."

"That would've been a good idea. Unfortunately, I have horses that need tending," Anne said.

"Oh how wonderful," said Gloria, excitedly. "I've always loved horses, but we just don't have the time or the space for them."

Anne looked at Zeke. "Maybe you could join us for dinner some night and you could meet them."

By the end of the evening, they had exchanged phone numbers and arranged to meet for dinner in two weeks when Sam and Gloria returned from vacation. They bade goodnight to their new friends and waited for the valet to bring the car.

✝

On the leisurely drive south on the Turquoise Trail, they talked animatedly about the new friends they'd met and some of the interesting eccentrics that seemed to flock to these society events.

Anne, thoroughly exhausted, held on to Zeke's arm as she rested her head against her shoulder. She inhaled the pleasant scent from Zeke's Vetiver cologne. The dashboard light reflected on the softly shadowed silhouette of Zeke's strong face. Anne moved closer and put her arm around Zeke's shoulders as she nestled into her neck softly kissing her. She slipped her hand inside Zeke's jacket.

"Zeke, I am so happy when I'm with you. And even though our relationship didn't have the ideal start, I can't imagine my life without you now. God knows what I would have done these past two weeks without your strength."

Zeke kissed Anne's forehead. "Well, for one thing you probably wouldn't have had the crap scared out of you."

Anne smiled. "I certainly don't blame you. Your job places you in harm's way and bad things sometimes happen." She hitched her fingers into the waistband of Zeke's slacks and hugged her closely.

Zeke rested her hand on Anne's thigh as they continued the long drive in comfortable silence.

†

"Boy, that bed sure is inviting," Anne, said. They climbed the stairs and entered the master bedroom. "I can't remember ever being this tired. Can we please stay in bed all day tomorrow?"

"There's nothing I would enjoy more." Zeke wiggled her eyebrows then leaned over to kiss Anne goodnight. Instead, she found herself lost in a kiss filled with longing and tenderness.

"I love you very much. I'm glad we're both okay and I hope we can put the ugliness behind us." Anne wove her fingers into the hair above Zeke's neck.

Zeke returned the kiss as she pulled Anne into her arms. In the dark, in the quiet, in the privacy of their bedroom, they kissed without haste. They kissed with a newer and even more mature passion. Their bodies molded together and moved in sync as if performing a mirror dance.

Inhale. Exhale. They were both breathing slowly and deeply uniting body, soul, and mind. They clung to each other and moved together as their pleasure intensified, thoughts were lost to exquisite sensations, and they peaked as one.

The kisses became softer and their touches from trembling fingertips grew lighter. They shared a few final whispers of love and fell into a blissful sleep.

Chapter Eighteen

A brief winter storm blew down from the northern mountains on Sunday. It hadn't been the first and wasn't surprising given it was the week before Thanksgiving. The cold weather provided the perfect opportunity to stay in, watch the snowfall, snuggle, and read the paper.

Monday morning was brisk and refreshing. Zeke held a fresh cup of coffee in her hand as she gazed out the kitchen window. Yesterday's lazy Sunday felt restorative, but the nightmares had also returned and left her restless and irritable.

She had slipped out of bed early and tried to call T.J. with no luck. She didn't think the schools were on vacation yet, so her friend was probably already at work.

Zeke unconsciously rubbed her temples acknowledging that the attack on Anne had frightened her. Waiting was no longer an option. This last attack from Hassan Hussein flipped a switch and she could no longer remain passive, especially when Anne was in danger.

Both Agent Hartbrooke in Chicago and Mike Donovan in Albuquerque knew about her recent encounter with Hussein. She needed to work out a plan to throw out a net large enough to ensnare some of the minor players, in an effort to catch Hassan. The information she had been sifting through revealed a network of individuals in several countries, directly or indirectly involved in various schemes involving drugs and money laundering. They were all loosely connected to the Hussein cartel. In order to do that, she needed a more secure Internet connection to access the other classified data sources available from federal intelligence agencies.

The house was quiet, and Zeke was restless. She listened then glanced at her watch as she stood at the foot of the stairs. Her heart rate picked up as she started up the stairs. It had been a long time since she had worried about someone.

Anne slept curled in a ball with the covers up to her ears. It was cruel to wake her, but Zeke was worried. She knelt beside the bed and carefully stroked a soft curl from Anne's forehead. "Annie," she whispered, "it's getting late. Are you working today?"

Anne's eyelids fluttered and blinked slowly, revealing clear blue eyes. A tiny smile creased sleep swollen lips. "Oh, hi," Anne groaned softly, "I called in sick. My head hurts."

One hand emerged from the covers, and Zeke kissed the palm. "Do you want me to get you something for the headache?"

"No, thank you. I'm just gonna sleep some more, 'kay?"

Zeke kissed her forehead. "Sure, you rest. I have some errands to run, but I'll have my cell phone." She watched the sleepy eyes close again and kissed her hand one last time before tucking it under the covers.

Her chest tightened as she closed the bedroom door. She felt like a criminal involving Anne in the ugliness that was part of her job. She sat down on the top step and pressed her fist against her forehead. Her mind began to spin like a gyroscope.

Problem solving had always been one of her strong suits, but this time it was different. She couldn't seem to get her feet under her. Everything was slipping away, and she didn't know how to hold on. Hot tears brimmed in her eyes. *What the fuck am I going to do?* Her cell phone vibrated, and she looked down at the text message.

Will be in the office all morning. Some new information is available. Mike

†

After meeting Zeke in the lobby, Agent Donovan brought them some coffee before they returned to the conference room.

Although she had texted him about the event in Phoenix, he asked Zeke to fill him in on the details.

"Wow, that was brazen. You sure it was Hassan?" Donovan stirred his coffee.

"He had a disguise, but I'm sure. I remember that face. I interviewed him in Chicago just as he was about to escape with his brother. As it turned out, he only hung around to stall us while Ahmed was boarding an international flight at Washington Dulles."

"And you're thinking there is a possibility that he wants revenge for his brother being sent to Gitmo?"

"I don't know what to think. I wasn't the one responsible. The CIA made the call and now I'm not sure what they've done. Hassan claimed his lawyers went to Cuba and there was no record of his brother. I asked Hartbrooke to check it out." Zeke swallowed hard to keep down the bile rising in her throat.

"This thing is getting out of hand. Can Hartbrooke help?"

Zeke nodded. "I talked to him. He's making some calls to some of his connections."

"I should talk to my boss. I mean, you're going to

be working here soon; she should be in the loop. Is your residence secure?" Mike scribbled a note.

"Fairly secure but, it's a friend's house in a gated community, she has a decent alarm system. But after this last attack in Phoenix, I don't know if anything's secure. He has good Intel and knows what we both look like. They also have my credit card info."

"The credit card info is easy enough. We'll order you new cards and purge the records. What about cars?"

Zeke felt her neck muscles tighten. "I'm still using the bureau loaner, but I plan to take the leased car back today and pick something different." She'd finished the coffee and was poking holes in the Styrofoam cup with her fingernail. "The first assault happened because the on-board GPS tracked our location. But recently, my friend told me she thought someone was following her. I planned to have her car checked but her mother died suddenly and we had to travel to Phoenix. I'm just not sure how much they've discovered or how soon we need to worry." *And I don't know what more they want from me!* The voice in her head screamed.

"I suppose we could give you new identities, but that wouldn't help us flush this guy out. I don't like it either but we need to know what he wants. I certainly think we can provide more security," said Donovan. "I have a friend, a retired agent, who does private security. I'll give you his number."

Zeke left the folder with the details she'd found on the Hussein connections. Donovan promised to let her know if he had anything new.

†

It was clear that both of their cars were posing a

threat so she decided to stop at a Subaru dealer. Zeke asked to see the sales manager.

"Good to see you, Ms. Cabot. Are you enjoying your stay?" the general manager asked.

Zeke grimaced. "Well, yes and no."

She explained that she was a federal agent working on a case and that the GPS identifier in her car had compromised her identity and location. He apologized profusely and offered to do whatever he could to make things right. She arranged to return on Tuesday with a friend to make a trade. She then thanked him and left.

After giving it a lot of thought, it seemed wise to avoid lease or other paper work. Zeke decided to arrange a transfer from her overseas account to pay for the transaction. Before leaving Albuquerque, Zeke stopped to pick up a pizza and six-pack of beer as well as a small bouquet of fresh flowers and a card. She was about to ask Anne to consider some major life style changes and she wanted to have her thoughts in order. It would be up to Anne whether or not she wanted to stay on the merry-go-round or settle in with more security.

The ordeal with her mother had been traumatic enough without the assault on the way home. Even though Zeke considered herself closed off emotionally, Anne was showing even more restraint and compartmentalization. She never talked about the assault. Anne hadn't reacted the way Zeke anticipated. *Maybe working as a nurse somehow has toughened her to outside forces.*

Her phone rang. "Cabot."

"Hey, buddy, I've only got a couple minutes before practice, but I wanted to call you. What's up?"

Zeke felt her shoulders relax hearing the sound of T.J.'s voice. "Hi, Teej, thanks for calling. I'm on my way home with a pizza and beer and enjoying a sunny drive through the canyon."

"Creep, we've got nine inches of snow and more coming tonight."

"Oh, yes, I remember the Windy City and the lake effect snow."

"Sure, just rub it in. How goes it with your beautiful lady?"

Zeke maneuvered her car into the right lane. "She's amazing, T.J.. We've had a rough week, but she's been a trooper." An image of Anne asleep on the bed popped into her mind.

"Don't tell me, another vicious snake attack?"

Zeke could hear T.J. chuckling. "No, she got some bad news last week. Her mother passed away suddenly, and we had to travel to Phoenix."

"I'm sorry. I didn't mean to be wise ass."

"I know. She didn't expect it." Zeke exited the interstate and pulled into a parking lot near a bank. "That's not all, though. When we were leaving Phoenix, the same guy that sent the goons that attacked us before, ambushed us at the rental car lot. We were both roughed up a little."

"Jesus! What the hell is this guy's problem?"

"I'm not really sure. If it was just me, I could handle it. Well, I could if I was working. But now Anne is involved, and I'm scared. T.J., I can't lose her, and I can't let anything else happen to her. I just don't know what to do. I don't know what they want from me. It's frustrating. My transfer was accepted, but I don't start work for another week and even though one of the agents is helping me, my hands are tied."

"Don't go off half cocked. If I know you, and I do, you won't sit back and wait for a fight. But I'm not sure you're ready to tangle with this dude. Z, I hope you remember why you went to New Mexico in the first place. You're on medical leave because your head's messed up. Do you understand that you may not be able to do this by yourself?"

The last remark hit home, and Zeke felt her throat burn with rage. "I know." There was a long pause because she couldn't express her fears aloud.

"It's okay, baby girl. You'll be all right. You just gotta get some help. Please, promise me you won't try to do this by yourself."

Zeke swiped at her eyes and swallowed. "Don't worry. I won't do anything foolish." But even though she said those words, she wasn't sure she knew what was foolish. "I better get home, the pizza is getting cold.

Zeke turned on North 14, and saw a billboard for the Georgia O'Keefe museum that reminded Zeke of the gala they attended. Anne had looked sensational and Zeke felt so proud, remembering how many admiring eyes had followed her that night. She wanted to protect that beautiful woman from any further danger at all costs.

The subdivision gate stood unexpectedly open, and Zeke made a mental note to ask about the security system and the neighborhood in general. As she drove along the winding road, she searched for danger spots. In a densely wooded area with homes so far apart, surveillance was difficult. When she reached Anne's driveway, she stopped and looked for places to mount surveillance cameras.

†

Anne was working in the kitchen when Zeke entered the house.

"Zeke, you startled me. I didn't hear your car."

"I'm sorry, hon. Maybe I should honk or something." Zeke handed Anne the flowers and kissed her.

"How sweet, I love flowers. Thanks, baby, and you brought pizza. I am so glad because I was drawing a blank on supper." Anne turned on the oven to warm the pizza. "How was your meeting with Agent Donovan?"

"It was good." Zeke placed the beer in the refrigerator. "And now we're on a first name basis, it's Mike."

"Mike, is it?" Anne ran her hand down Zeke's back.

"Yes, and he's quite handsome in a military sort of way. It suits him along with his wife and two little girls." Zeke winked.

"What did you two figure out?" Anne continued cleaning up the sink and counter.

"I filled him in on our encounter in Phoenix. He said he'd send an email to the Phoenix field office to see what they had turned up. If they can find the driver, who must be one of Hussein's men, we might have a solid lead. We also talked a little about more security for you and me."

"Security? What for? Are we in danger?"

Anne turned to face Zeke, her face blanched and the fear returned to her eyes. It was something Zeke never wanted to see again.

"There's no indication of any threat. It's simply a precaution," Zeke said. "I need to get some new credit cards and be more careful. Now that we've been recognized, there is a possibility that these characters might still want trouble."

Zeke walked to the refrigerator, grabbed two bottles of beer, and twisted the caps off. She handed one to Anne and kissed her cheek reassuringly.

"I also think it might be wise for both us to trade our cars for different models." She watched for reaction. This suggestion was more than a little more security. Anne's life had been turned side down since they met. Cautions like this probably felt a little cloak and dagger. Zeke didn't have time to do this gradually. Hassan Hussein could be in Albuquerque right now. "I will be glad to handle the arrangements so there will be no paper trail."

Anne was looking more apprehensive, and Zeke reached for her hand and led her into the den and the couch. "Honey, I know this all sounds dramatic and maybe unnecessary. I hope it is, but I also want us to be safe."

"I can't say you didn't warn me about the dangers, but my, God, you're not even working yet."

"I know. This is all blowback because of the Chicago case. Nobody wishes it were over more than I do and maybe it is. Mike Donovan is really the one who made the suggestions about security. He even offered us witness protection." Zeke tried to smile.

"What?"Anne sat up straighter. "Are you serious?"

"It was just a thought. I think we're fine with some basic precautions." Zeke decided to hold back the idea of surveillance cameras for the time being and changed the subject. "When do you need to go back to work?"

Anne stood and returned to the kitchen to clear off the table. "Not until next week. Right now I don't feel much like listening to patients."

Zeke brought out some plates and napkins. "I was wondering, do you think they could find something for you to do in the office for a while. You know, instead of bouncing around in a car all day. At least ride the desk until we can get the car squared away?" Zeke hoped to keep Anne out of the public eye for as long as possible without alarming her.

"I'll call tomorrow and ask my boss," said Anne.

After enjoying the pizza, they went for a short walk down the road to enjoy the fall colors as the evening shadows lengthened on the mountainside. Anne described what little she knew of the neighbors as Zeke made mental notes. The subdivision seemed secure, but Anne's property was still vulnerable on the east side because it was rough terrain on a steep hill with limited visibility. It would be easy to access the house from that side. Video surveillance was necessary, so she would contact Mike in the morning.

Zeke tried hard to let go of the cascading worries and what-ifs. They walked arm in arm sharing warmth and closeness. It felt good to enjoy these quiet moments, especially after the trauma they each had endured. The adrenaline-fueled drama had drained them both and shared moments like this restored them.

Chapter Nineteen

During a long conversation over dinner, Zeke had explained to Anne the value of upgrading the security system by adding just a *few* cameras and some software. The car idea required more delicate negotiating and more promises, but Zeke convinced Anne to trade her car.

The explanation of the financial shell game took until bedtime. Zeke had a lawyer create a shell company through a connection in Lucerne, Switzerland named "AnZc Ltd., LLC". She then also opened a bank account for the corporation in Albuquerque, which provided her with checking, savings, and credit cards. A check from this bank would cover the cost of the cars with title and registration in the company name. Hopefully, this would provide them with another layer of security.

The next day they each drove in to Albuquerque to meet with the sales manager at the Subaru dealership. Anne insisted on a pre-owned red Forester with only 1200 miles. Zeke chose a new silver Legacy. The car dealer offered her a good deal because of his embarrassment about the GPS debacle and the inducement of selling two cars at one time for cash.

They stood in the parking lot admiring their new cars.

"I really like it," Anne said. "We have to talk about this money situation. I'm not letting you buy me a car. I'm not destitute and you do not 'owe' me."

Zeke finally relented and agreed that the car cost

would cover her share of expenses for the house, utilities, insurance, and the dreaded security system. She put an arm around Anne's shoulders. "I wasn't trying to upset you. I did this for security. We can talk about banking and the corporation later. It was the smart thing to do, and you can talk with your accountant tomorrow if you'd like. Right now, let's go home."

†

Zeke sat down on the couch next to Anne once the new cars were safe in the garage. "Annie, what would you like to do for Thanksgiving?"

The question stunned Anne. "I have no idea. I lost track of time. I didn't realize it was so soon." *Where did the past week go?* Her thoughts spun wildly. She turned and looked into Zeke's eyes, which stilled the buzzing.

"Yup, it's the day after tomorrow. Do you have any traditions you like to follow or would you like to go out?" Zeke tenderly traced her finger across Anne's forehead.

Anne flashed back on years past when she and Andrew would host an annual holiday open house. The holidays were something she enjoyed especially decorating and planning the menu. At one time, Anne Reynolds reigned as the premier hostess. Where had that witty outgoing person disappeared? She reached over and grasped Zeke's hand. "I wish we had a group of friends that we could invite over and entertain—we could tell stories and laugh, eat a deliciously decadent meal, and drink expensive wine."

"What about the doctor friend you met in Santa Fe? Maybe they'd be free?"

Anne brightened briefly then faded. "When they

talked about getting together, they said it would have to be after their vacation trip over Thanksgiving."

"If it were up to me, I would be just as thankful eating peanut butter sandwiches and watching movies with you," Zeke pulled Anne close and kissed her softly.

Anne responded immediately. Her pulse quickened as she returned the kiss. "Oh, baby, me too. We can stay in and I'll pick up a small turkey and fixings."

"You decide. I would be happy to take you to the finest restaurant in town and show you off, if you'd rather." Zeke raked her fingers through Anne's hair as she brushed her lips across Anne's neck.

Anne cuddled closer enjoying the warmth of Zeke's body. Reluctantly she said, "Do you wanna fix supper or feed the horses?"

†

It was already dark when Zeke finished with the horses. She ducked into the garage and retrieved the large halogen MagLite from the glove box of her car. Trying to be quiet, she walked over to the south side the house. The leaves had fallen steadily for a couple of weeks and made it difficult to move quietly. Technicians had positioned small cameras on the house and some motion sensor lights across the wooded eastern slope, according to Zeke's instructions.

Motion sensors activated high tech digital cameras that we on the corners of the house and linked to her computer that she backed up on an external hard drive each night. There was also a satellite uplink so a private security firm could monitor the property if they were away. And, Zeke made sure wired glass break sensors were on each window and door.

Zeke felt safer having the system, the workings of which were not something Anne needed to know right now. From her position just east of the house, she could see Anne standing at the sink and she shuddered to think how easy it would be— *Stop it.* Zeke felt a warm tug at her heart watching Anne preparing a meal for them. The down side of love was the fear of losing that special someone. Zeke strengthened her resolve to extricate herself from the Hussein cartel case and hopefully pass it up the chain of command to another agency.

Zeke returned to the house after the walk-about. She would check the monitor later to see if her presence had registered.

Chapter Twenty

Wednesday morning arrived with more snow covering the evergreens with a magical dusting of confection. Sunlight glistened off the ice crystals adorning the large evergreens. A silent blanket covered the world as Zeke lay on her side close behind Anne watching the snowfall on the tall trees outside the window.

Her childhood in Biloxi was not a White Christmas world. It was the Deep South with warm Gulf winds and Mississippi traditions. As matriarch in the family, her grandmother was responsible for the holidays. Even though her family was small, her grandmother would invite 'strays' as she called them, to any holiday meal.

Zeke smiled at the memory of her round petite grandmother standing on her porch in a gingham apron with a dishtowel in her hands. She welcomed each guest to her humble celebration. The food was plentiful, and after dinner, they enjoyed songs and stories. It was a happier time, a simpler time. When was it that things began to fracture and they each went their own way? She wasn't sure but guessed it was when her grandmother died. Nobody even tried to carry on her traditions.

Zeke certainly had traveled a long and tortuous road to the bed she now shared with this fair-haired woman in the mountains of New Mexico. The gently falling snowflakes mesmerized her. Zeke sighed deeply and relished the warm sensation engulfing her heart. The faint smell of lilies of the valley mixed with

Anne's unique scent filled her.

She slipped from the bed reluctantly and dressed quietly then stepped out to boot up her computer. The more she settled in to her new life, the more she wanted to close the chapter of her life tainted by the Hussein family. She knew there was a missing link. Too much money moved through Hassan's import business which didn't have that many sales—at least their tax returns didn't show it.

Hassan easily spent half the year traveling and visiting many of the cities repeatedly: Beirut, Qandahar, Karachi, Dubai, then across the African continent to Gambon, Senegal, across the Atlantic to Venezuela, Bogota, El Salvador, Oaxaca and Guyamas, and Mexico. Zeke placed markers on the map on her computer using Google earth. She studied the mental lines between the various destinations searching for a pattern or common denominator. Artifacts? Drugs? Contraband? It could be any of a thousand things, and it certainly kept Hassan busy. What was the connection that made him interrupt his schedule to track her down? Ahmed Hussein held the key but she had no idea where the CIA had taken him.

†

An hour later, Anne emerged from the bedroom with tousled hair, wearing a worn tee shirt looking sleepy and delicious. She leaned over the back of the chair wrapping her arms around Zeke sighing contentedly. "Let's go out for dinner tomorrow and maybe see a show."

Zeke turned in the chair and pulled Anne onto her lap. "That sounds like a great idea." They lingered over a kiss as Zeke's brain began to disengage from maps and travel routes. The electrical pathway between her lips ignited and the on switch lit up. Anne's warm body and her tender lips became a wonderful distraction.

Anne stopped abruptly. "Okay, I didn't mean to take you away from your work. I'll shower and leave you alone." One more long wet kiss and Anne disappeared into the bedroom.

Zeke opened her browser and noticed the flashing of an instant message. It was from Hartbrooke and simply said, "Call me on secure line." She pulled out her cell phone and scrolled down to the number he provided on her last visit.

"Hartbrooke."

"It's Cabot, sir. You messaged me?"

"Yes, good afternoon. I just got off the phone with a contact at Langley. He verified that they transferred Ahmed Hussein to Guantanamo Bay last night. Prior to that, he had apparently been at an undisclosed location in North Africa."

Zeke sagged back in her chair. "That's odd, but good news. Now, if his brother checks, he'll know I was telling the truth. Is there any way to get that news to Hussein's lawyers?"

"Not a bad idea. I'll have someone pass it on to the district attorney. They're practically on a first name basis with those lawyers. Enjoy your holiday, Agent Cabot."

"You too sir, thanks for the news."

What a relief. Zeke hung up, put the phone on the desk, and pumped her fist in the air. Maybe those expensive attorneys could work some magic, but either way, she could think of no reason that Hussein would have any more interest in her. *Hallelujah.*

After copying the maps and other data, she backed

up her computer and shut it down. She walked down stairs and found Anne in the library curled up with a book. She sat on the footstool and repositioned Anne's legs across her lap. "Whatcha doin'?"

"Trying to be quiet and read."

"Am I disturbing you?" Zeke leaned close to Anne's ear.

Anne placed the book face down on her lap and sighed. She looked stern but her eyes twinkled. "Yes. But I can't resist you, Zeke Cabot. Why are you pestering me?" She leaned forward to receive a kiss.

Zeke obliged. "I talked to Hartbrooke and he confirmed that Hussein was recently transferred to Guantanamo Bay. If Hassan checks, he'll find I was telling the truth."

Anne clapped her hands together. "That's wonderful, so we won't have any more ugly surprises?"

"I hope not. I'd really like to close that chapter once and for all. Also, I talked to Agent de la Hoya earlier and I will officially be starting work on Monday."

Anne stuck out her lower lip. "Poop."

"I know, but my leave is over and I've reached a point in my research where I will need some better tools like the agency's computers. It's a little safer to be snooping on a secure server."

"Are you doing something dangerous?" Anne's eyebrows furrowed causing worry lines on her forehead.

Zeke hated that look. "No, darlin', I'm just following up on some old information and trying to tie it together. Analysts do that type of work all the time—in the office—not in the field. I'm safe."

The worry lines began to fade and Anne leaned forward wrapping her arms around Zeke's neck. "In that case, you may go, as long as you remember to come home to me."

†

On Thursday, they dressed to the nines and headed into Albuquerque for dinner and a show at the Sandia Resort and Casino located at the base of the Sandia Mountains. Zeke had never been to a casino and was looking forward to trying her luck.

Anne did some research and told Zeke that the tribal members of the Sandia pueblo owned and operated the recently built four-star hotel. Today they offered a full Thanksgiving buffet and wine prix fixe. There were four entrees to choose from including the traditional turkey with all the trimmings. Dozens of elegant choices lined the dessert table. Not surprisingly, families crowded the dining room while the staff worked hard clearing used plates and serving the extras.

Zeke and Anne lingered almost two hours over unimaginable choices before forcing themselves to stand and walk around the casino. By late afternoon, the sun warmed the earth and began to melt the small amount of snow that had accumulated.

The snow adorning trees high on the Sandia's remained pristine and sparkling in the early winter sun. There was no breeze, which made it comfortable to stand on the patio and gaze at the steep rocky crags facing the mesas several miles west of them. The ragged western face of the Sandia's was markedly different from the view of the east side with its gradual slope, dense with piñon, juniper, and scrub oak.

"You know," Zeke began rather pensively, "I really like New Mexico. It has a desolate and ancient kind of beauty. And I'm really glad I stumbled into

230

you."

"I completely agree with you, and I'm glad you stumbled, too. The ten-dollar bribe to that evil snake was well worth it."

Zeke poked Anne in the ribs, and they both laughed.

They remained on the patio until the air grew chilly. The "Motown Review" started at six p.m. and they moved toward the theater to find their seats.

†

Zeke and Anne spent the remainder of the holiday weekend on adjusting to merging their lives, even as they continued the adventure of discovering each other's idiosyncrasies. Zeke knew that when two adult women, who are both a bit headstrong and set in their ways, begin to cohabitate, inevitable conflicts occur. On a couple of occasions, they had already had to take a break, cool down then sit together and discuss a workable solution.

"Not everyone enjoys laundry or cleaning bathrooms or mucking stalls," Anne explained.

They made compromises.

Never having owned a home, the number of responsibilities that went along with it astounded Zeke. Even more difficult was the division of financial responsibility.

Anne resisted Zeke's attempts to pay for things. After all, in addition to her salary, according to her, Anne received a healthy alimony check as well as money from her mother's untapped assets.

For the same reason, Zeke had no qualms about spending the money that she squirreled away for fifteen years of government service. She made some very sound investments early on, which had quadrupled in value.

Neither was destitute, and both eventually negotiated an equitable agreement. They established a household account to which they both contributed and Zeke agreed that Anne would manage it.

†

At the end of the day and after two glasses of wine, they toasted the mutual commitment to live together in a long-term relationship. Cheers.

Anne was thrilled and surprisingly, so was Zeke. After the turmoil and uncertainty of the past two months, they both yearned for and rejoiced in a sense of stability.

At Zeke's urging, Anne arranged to return to work in the office for the time being. The director agreed since one of the telemedicine nurses was going to take maternity leave in two weeks. Telemedicine had become an essential part of Home Health Care because of the vast amount of territory in their treatment area. Many of the patients lived over fifty miles from a hospital or a doctor and being able to have a nurse as close as the phone for a video visit where the patient could have heart, lungs, blood glucose and oxygen levels checked, changed lives.

Anne was ready for a change and a challenge. She was tired of worrying about safety and she was tired of obsessing about what she might have done to prevent her mother's sudden death. In the end, there was nothing she could do; it was tragic and a waste. At the heart of it all, she loved her mother and missed her and it saddened her that her mother didn't have the opportunity to meet Zeke and know how truly happy her daughter had become.

†

"Annie? Where are you?"

"In the laundry room."

Zeke trotted downstairs and pulled her jacket from a peg in the mudroom. "I'm going to walk down the road and back before lunch. Thought I'd better check in with T.J."

"Okay, hon, we'll eat when you get back."

Zeke opened the front door to find a woman with a basket in her hand. "Hello."

The woman smiled. "You must be Zeke. My name is Susan. I'm Anne's next-door neighbor. I've been dying to meet you."

"It's nice to meet you," Zeke said. "Please come in. I was just going out for a few minutes but I'll be right back. Anne's in the laundry room."

"Oh, you go ahead. I'll find Anne."

So that's Susan. Zeke started down the walk and looked over her shoulder. The air was crisp and the smell of piñon smoke lingered in the air.

She hit speed dial after pulling out her Bluetooth.

"Hey Zeke, perfect timing. We just finished lunch. To what do I owe this honor?"

"T.J., My dear old friend, for the first time I am calling you without complaint or worry."

"Oh, Lord, are you drunk?"

This time it was Zeke's turn to laugh. "No my friend, my life is good. My life is better than good. It's exquisite. Tomorrow I start a new job and my beautiful partner will be safely working in an office. I think I have enough evidence to get my nemesis arrested. And I've never been more in love with anyone in my life."

"Praise be. You have no idea how long I have waited to hear those words."

"Yeah I do. I'm almost afraid to say it; I think I may have found the one person I was meant to be with forever. Anne just seems to 'get' me. I wasn't sure this could ever happen with—well you know, all the stuff going on. Every morning I wake up and think maybe I've been dreaming."

"You deserve it, you deserve to be happy. And, listen don't screw this up. Keep your heart open and trust."

Zeke stopped and took a deep breath. "You're right. I still feel a little skeptical...you know, waiting for the other shoe to drop."

"That's understandable, but sooner or later you have to trust somebody. Hey, Cheryl, guess what?" T.J. shouted.

Zeke chuckled at her friend's enthusiasm. "Okay, okay. You guys can celebrate. I'm going home to enjoy a home cooked meal with my beloved. I'll give you a call next week."

"I'm really happy for you. I love you, girl friend."

"I love you too, T.J., say hi to Cheryl."

In spite of the chill in the air, Zeke felt her heart overflowing with love.

†

"Susan, this is beautiful." Anne carefully removed a blueberry pie from the basket.

"I made two of them this year as a surprise, but turns out the boys don't like blueberry. We had to go to Jim's folks for Thanksgiving so I didn't get a chance to come over sooner." Susan sat down at the kitchen counter as Anne handed her a glass of wine.

"I'm sure Zeke will be thrilled because I'm not much of a baker and this smells heavenly."

"So, I met the elusive girlfriend at the door."

Anne looked up as a blush warmed her cheeks. "Oh?"

"Yes, and she is every bit as attractive as you told me. Really, she's beautiful and very polite. Can I assume that things are going well?"

The warmth now covered her face and neck. "Oh, Susan, I don't think I've ever been as happy as I have the last few weeks. We've certainly had our struggles." She didn't feel it was the time to talk about her mother's sudden death. She brought her wine glass over to the counter and sat down. "Zeke has been a Godsend. I don't know what I would've done without her."

Susan touched her wineglass with Anne's glass. "I don't think I've seen you looking this happy in years." She laughed. "Honey, you're glowing."

Anne touched her face with her fingers and felt the heat—the new heat generated by Zeke's presence in her life. It was uncomfortable, but in a good way.

The front door opened, and along with Zeke, a gust of cold air blew in the room.

"It's me, sorry about the north wind."

"We're in the kitchen, come have some wine with us," Anne said.

Zeke appeared in the doorway from the dining room. Her wavy hair looked windblown and her cheeks slightly burnished from the cold, but Zeke's smile lit up the room. Anne had never felt prouder.

"Susan, I'd like to introduce my girlfriend, Zeke Cabot."

✝

Anne returned later that afternoon from running errands in town to find Zeke busily working in the barn. She had mucked out the stalls and spread new straw, cleaned and filled the water tank and was stacking the new hay. Anne walked to the corral fence with a huge grin on her face as warmth flooded her heart. At that moment, she felt like they were an actual 'couple'.

Zeke didn't see her at first and continued moving the heavy bales; her shirt was damp and clinging to her body. She grunted to lift the bales over her head. To Anne's eyes, she had never looked hotter or more delicious. She felt herself flushing with a mixture of love and desire. Zeke stopped and stepped back to admire her work as she wiped her face with her sleeve. She turned slowly and waved. She smiled revealing that elusive dimple.

Anne opened the gate and joined her in the hay barn. "Damn you look hot, woman." Anne ran her hands up the denim shirtfront as Zeke cupped Anne's ass tightly with her gloved hands and pulled her close providing a soft, tender kiss and embrace.

Zeke's persistent and entreating mouth elicited a deep groan from Anne's throat, and her arms encircled Zeke's strong shoulders. Her hips pressed forward. Their greeting heated up and Anne decided to take it indoors.

"Do you want some lunch?" Anne watched Zeke remove her boots and jeans in the garage.

"Not right now, I really want to shower this smell off."

"I like that smell," Anne protested. Anything to do with horses was pleasurable for Anne.

Zeke laughed and hurried upstairs to clean up.

Anne hung up her jacket and turned on the radio but couldn't get the vision of the sweaty cowgirl out of her mind. She headed upstairs with a plan. After digging out an old quilt, she found her massage oil.

When Zeke exited the master bath wrapped in a towel, Anne beckoned with her hand. "Come on over here, cowgirl. I think a hard working woman like you might need a massage to keep those muscles from tightening up."

"Yes, ma'am." Zeke smiled and sauntered to the bed discarding the towel, and stretching out across the foot of the bed on her stomach.

Anne poured some of the almond oil into her palm and rubbed her hands together. She then started her massage with long slow strokes up Zeke's back along the spinal column and gently back down the sides.

Zeke groaned with pleasure.

Anne repeated her ministrations varying pressure, which elicited a variety of guttural sounds from Zeke. She worked the shoulders and arms slowly and gently while admiring the glistening skin that looked like bronze.

Anne moved down to her feet and legs where she massaged the middle, outside and inner legs in long strokes, one at a time. Each foot and toe was firmly kneaded and squeezed, evoking a very satisfied, 'oh yes' from Zeke.

Anne nudged Zeke to roll over on her back. Looking down on the naked and vulnerable body, Anne found herself distracted by her lust but quickly moved up and knelt behind Zeke's head where she stroked her beautiful face and hair. She ran her fingers across Zeke's forehead, cheekbones, jaw line, and nose. Anne reached under and held her head while she massaged her neck and shoulders.

One arm at a time, Anne stroked and worked the forearms and each hand with her thumbs applying more oil. She gently ran her hands across Zeke's flat belly, up her sides and down across her breasts, kneading them gently.

Zeke was totally relaxed and pliable. Evidently, a little aroused as her legs moved apart.

Anne's pulse increased as her own body began to respond to Zeke's arousal. Adding more oil, she reached down to massage both thighs moving closer and closer to the apex. Zeke moaned deeply and grasped the bedspread in her clenched fists.

She continued to stroke slowly and lightly moving her fingers using a circular motion and looked at Zeke as she cried out sending rhythmic spasms rippling across her body until she wilted with relief.

After she finished, Anne stretched onto the bed next to Zeke and watched the rapid beat of Zeke's heart in her neck artery. Zeke was spent.

Anne smiled at the beautiful body lying beside her. "You are exquisite. Do you know that? I think I'm going to quit my job so I can stay home and play massage therapist with you all day."

Zeke rolled onto her side. "I don't think that's a good idea. You have completely drained me. I feel as weak as a kitten, but I really enjoyed your massage. I've never had one."

"Seriously?"

"Never." Zeke crossed her naked breast with her finger.

"Well, we must see to it that we schedule you again real soon." Anne ran her tongue across Zeke's lower lip and reached her hand around the back of Zeke's neck, cradled her head, and kissed her deeply.

They lay facing one another.

Zeke ran her finger along Anne's neck lifting the gold chain. She held the gold Pegasus charm in her palm. "Do you remember when I gave this to you?"

Anne touched it with her finger. "Yes, it was the day you left to go back to Chicago. I cried as I watched your plane takeoff. And every night I went to sleep holding this charm. Just like making love with you, flying horses have a way of lifting us above all the pain and strife." She kissed Zeke. "With you I feel like I'm flying sometimes, it really is like defying gravity and soaring to a place of pure bliss."

Zeke pulled her close and held her tightly, "I love you, Annie, and I'm blessed to have found you."

About the Author

Barrett

Act I

The fable of Barrett began in the suburbs of Chicago where she and her younger brother filled their summers with fanciful playacting and story telling. (Not one single electronic game in sight.) Fast forward to high school and college, where a foundation was laid in English, theater, and art. After an adventurous year living in Hollywood, scrounging a living and the theatrical career path took a sharp detour when a wise teacher suggested including a day job to support the dream.

Act II

Back to the Midwest. A brief stint as a nurse's aide ignited a new passion-- for medicine. In thirty-five years as a registered nurse, she amassed a treasure trove of information about bureaucracy, hospitals, human nature, trauma, and the indomitable human spirit. She enjoyed twenty years in Wisconsin, where she worked in the local ER, a surgical practice and created a successful allergy/environmental practice for fifteen years.

Some of that time was also spent priming her right brain by studying and making jewelry, assemblage, and photographing everything. Many of the photographs came from travels in the US, Scotland, Ireland, France, the former USSR, Mexico and Belize.

Act III

Now retired in the high desert of New Mexico, Barrett re-created herself as a writer. Seizing this new opportunity with characteristic zeal—she hammered out first drafts for ten manuscripts in four years. The challenge of the storytelling and the craft has reawakened childhood imagination and now the sky's the limit.

E-Books, Limited First Edition Print, Printed Books, Free e-books

Visit our website for more publications available online.

http://www.affinityebooks.com

Published by Affinity E-Book Press NZ Ltd

Canterbury, New Zealand

Registered company 2517228

Made in the USA
Lexington, KY
18 September 2012